# The Party at Twin Oaks Ranch

*Hi Al!*
*Part of this book is dedicated*
*To You and Part to Stuart*
*Love*
by
*DAD*

# Don Campbell

**AmErica House**
**Baltimore**

First printing

ISBN: 1–58851–191–X
PUBLISHED BY AMERICA HOUSE BOOK PUBLISHERS
www.publishamerica.com
Baltimore

Printed in the United States of America

# Chapter 1

I was filing my last story of the day.

It was hardly earth shaking—and difficult.

It shouldn't have been.

It was the "fluff stuff" about a wayward cat "Charla" that crawled up under a car engine. Owner started the car, Charla let out a screech and tumbled out bleeding and crying. An overworked small town veterinarian sewed her up with 100 stitches, splinted her broken leg, and patched her half–chewed ear.

It was light and hardly mind–boggling. I don't know why it was so hard to write. It was the kind of feature story that you usually put together in minutes, but now I had sat on it for 45 minutes. I erased dozens of words on the terminal, substituted others with a touch of a button. Somehow the words didn't match the ideas.

Deadlines had long passed. Everything was wrapped up on the Daily *Oakland Herald*. The whole newsroom seemed asleep. The zip had gone out of the day. Reporters dozed at their little black screens with the green words spilling out. A lot of looking but not much output. A combination of mid winter doldrums and long, cold days in Michigan that seemed to never end at this time of year had put everyone in deep freeze. In Michigan the weather reaches its winter peak in February; March is up and down, and in April you look for a spring that never seems to arrive until May.

I couldn't even force my tired, end–of–the–day brain to function. It rambled out of control. I was helpless to command it, like a blade of grass that bent forward or backward, or sideways, according to which way the wind blew.

The Kaleidoscopic picture was suddenly taking me back in time to when the Herald newsroom installed their first computer typesetters a few years ago. I don't know why the moment was on recall except that it was a very important historical point in time.

"Bastard Reporting" the older newsmen had said. "Never work. Damn computers are taking over the world—and now the newsroom."

But prejudice was soon overcome. Reporters composed at a much higher rate of speed than on typewriters. A command button automatically erased words, transposed lines, slugged in your name, and did a lot of other things. Progress, in spite of opposition, was here to stay.

Each reporter now filed his stories in a "Memory Box." You could recall the story with a flick of a button. No endless files of news clippings no bulging folders you only had to push a command button and hundreds of little green words popped upon your video screen.

Marvelous.

Amazing.

Let's face it. The age of green eye shades, tipped up hat brims, the sound of "Hold the Press," and assignment sheets all had departed and gone the way of the clanking hot lead linotype, the heavily weighted zinc photographic plates, and the high pitched scream of a Hammond saw cutting linotype slugs, all slithering into the oblivion of newspaper's yesterdays.

Now, editors looked at summary sheets of stories, neatly spewed out by a computer and determined their news priority. Reporters sometimes made up their own headlines, type length all neatly measured by a computer. A "floppy disk" computer had memory files of every story written. A long cry from the old "Morgue file" that took up a whole room.

A classified Ad taker not only typed out her ad but also programmed it into a computer for billing. She even had a command button that could tell her, while taking down an ad, whether the customer was up on his credit rating.

Ah, the age of computers.

Absently, I wondered how old man Horace Greeley, the flamboyant editor of the "Good Old Days" would have managed today. Pushing just one button and having hundreds of words spill out probably would have short–circuited the old boy's memory box. His green eyeshade probably would have turned two shades of purple.

Onward and upward.

Somehow I found the necessary words to complete the story. The phrasing was awkward and the sentences rambling. I thought how terribly disappointed my old professor at Michigan State University would have been to see such "garbage."

With hardly any feeling I filed the story into "memory" half expecting to see when I called up, a one–word command in caps, "REDO."

With shortsighted optimism I secretly hoped there would be a follow up story on Charla where I could do better. Maybe she would regain her damaged sex life and father a big family in spite of her traumatic experience and severe injuries. Now that would be a story….

This jangling of my desk phone interrupted my thoughts.

"Hello," I muttered absently. "Mike Dunn of the Herald." My mind was still focusing on Charla's sex life.

"This is Deputy Sheriff Fred Hansard," the voice said. "Mike, I think we've got something you will be interested in here."

Sheriff Hansard's face came into sharp focus on my brain. He was a lean, lanky guy. Talked frequently with a cigarette hanging out of his mouth. A longtime law enforcement officer he was thoroughly professional, and inclined to believe that lawmen were straight from heaven. I honestly thought Hansard felt that if God were to revisit the earth he would come as a police officer. He left nothing to chance; carried a tape measure with him constantly and at the scene of a crime was out measuring car skid tracks, footprints, etc., down to the last 1/16 of an inch. He was thorough, coldly scientific and a professional lawman in every sense.

I had known him for some time as a friend and he frequently helped me on breaking stories. A newspaperman without his sources is dead in the water.

His words came out crisp and clear.

"We found a young, 15–year–old white male dead in a field, apparently died of exposure. No major bruises or such to indicate death was by homicide but certainly under suspicious circumstances."

Why are all police reports the same, I thought. Someone is a white or black male or female. Then you run through phrasing like… "a black male suspect was seen fleeing the scene of the crime. Footprints indicated the suspect fled to a nearby 1981 white Cadillac four–door sedan. Two white, male witnesses said the Cadillac fled the scene at a very high rate of speed, narrowly missing a southbound vehicle driven by a white female."

Why can't policemen write in more glamorous, exciting language; maybe like a "curly haired man with a surly sneer, and livid scar on his left cheek, walking with a slight limp, was seen mysteriously talking to a stranger in a rumpled trench coat, near the scene of the crime?"

But, I argued, "you jerk, policemen are supposed to be scientific, they aren't supposed to be double ought seven characters."

My mind jerked back to the present and I said: "Where is the body of this 15 year old white male located?"

I couldn't help throwing in some police talk to make it sound like I was really a part of the system. I rolled the words out slowly, maybe even embellishing them.

"In Whitfield Township, just north of Jaspar and Springfield Roads," said Hansard. He added: "the body looks in real rough shape, has been out in a field for three or four days. Medical Examiner is out there now. It's not too far from your paper and you might want to check on it. Apparently, the kid wandered away from a teenage drinking party," he added.

I thanked him for the tip and hung up, my mind racing. No homicide indicated, he said, but certainly worth more than an ordinary obit notice.

It needed investigation and was a lot more interesting than Charla's escape from death. On top of that the afternoon was still young and I had most of tomorrow's stories already written. It seemed like an appropriate time for the young, enterprising reporter to go to work. I checked in with my managing editor and he agreed.

It was one of those dreary, cloud–filled days in Michigan, the kind you see in late February. Midway between winter and spring the weather is a boring mixture of thaw and ice. The temperature is like an escalator, either on the way rapidly upward or down. Nothing is constant. Extremes are not hard to find.

I stepped into my beat up Mustang, banged the starter, and held my breath as the engine slowly churned, and churned, in the frigid temperature. Then it caught, miraculously, and I thought, "Thank God, no starter cables this time."

Coughing constantly, with an occasional belch of smoke from a backfire, I wheeled the Mustang northward on Interstate 85, taking an exit into the Village of Whitfield, a neat little community with nice, clean, old fashioned houses and a business section of sturdy two story brick buildings that sprawled out over nearly two miles.

One thing you can't miss in the town is its quaint, uncluttered look, and old–fashioned courtesy and hospitality. A motorist passing through is impressed with buildings and homes that know no shape or size. No sir, no rectangular shaped, all–the–same buildings that you see in a shopping center or look–alike subdivision; that you go through hardly knowing or sensing they are there. Whitfield COMMANDS to be seen. It calls to you. Your curiosity is whetted and you must investigate.

Whitfield was my hometown before I went to Journalism school and then got a job on a "big city newspaper." I love the town, in fact, had spent some time on the weekly Whitfield Gazette before taking up with the Herald. Some of my links are still there. The "twofers" (2–for–the–price–of–one) drinks at the old Whitfield Hotel carry fond memories of literally "crawling" home to my old fashioned aunt's place where I stayed after the sudden death of my parents. Usually she was waiting up and a stern lecture followed that I was headed for the role of "town drunk" unless I mended my ways. Then the next morning she filled me with steamy hot cakes, eggs, and bacon as if to ask my forgiveness by overstuffing me.

One of the big moments in history claimed by Whitfield is when Carry Nation, the famed booze battler, came to town and gave a lecture on temperance at the Old Opera House in the 1900's and then proceeded to walk down the town's saloon–laden street, sweeping off all the liquor bottles from the bars with her parasol. The town fathers had called that street "Battle Alley" because of the many brawls that took place there on Saturday night after the town bullies had completed a round of the saloons.

Complete with Bordello girls, the town lush, singing bar-tenders, and an appearance by the Women's Christian Temperance Union, the town stages a festival each year pointing out the sins of booze and corruption. And, although the theme of the festival centers on these two unforgivable sins, there is a spirited battle to see who will get the permits to sell beer and wine to the thousands of tourists who visit the town. The fathers explained away the seeming conflict in philosophy, saying that the proceeds are used for local charitable projects, an act that even old Carry would probably sanction.

As the Mustang asymmetrically made its way down Jasper Road I noticed a group of people gathered around a fence–row. As I approached, their faces appeared tense and foreboding, a reflection of disaster. They were gathered around a plastic pouch that had already been zipped up and was about to be dispatched to the morgue by a waiting ambulance.

There was the smell of death about—a smell I had grown used to over my years of reporting; a sweet scent, overpowering and pungent.

It always brought to my mind other sad experiences with death: a home where four elderly people died in grotesque, ghoulish positions—on the davenport, the chair and the basement, after a leaky furnace overcame them; a fisherman who drowned and wasn't found for six months; an old lady who wondered away from a rest home and expired in a field and now a young teenager dead of exposure in a pasture, from certainly suspicious circumstances.

The flashback ended suddenly and I knew I had to get to work. Rationally, my mind set an organized routine, one that I recalled for times like this. I had plenty of time, if I needed it; deadlines are always in the back of your mind on something like this and I had until 10:30 a.m. the next day to get the story together. It now looked like it could be front page; a young boy found in a cow pasture under mysterious circumstances and motives, a suspicion that he had wandered away from a teenage drinking party, and a questionable death. I wanted to make sure everything was tied up before it got to the print stage.

I started in on Deputy Hansard.

"What's it all about, Fred," I asked.

"This young, 15–year–old white male—"

"Cut the police crap, Fred," I interrupted, "give it to me straight on."

"Okay," he said, "This young kid was last seen at a teenage party at Twin Oaks Ranch three nights ago. Name's Tommy Furman. His parents filed a Missing Persons report on him the next morning when he didn't show up. Things are pretty sketchy right now and we're still investigating as to motive, if there is one," he said. He added there was considerable drinking going on at the party."

"What happens now?" I asked.

"Well, we start checking on his movements at the party, the coroner's office runs an autopsy, we get blood samples, do some interviewing and then maybe we'll get some answers."

"Looks like you're on hold, now. Let me check back with you first thing in the morning after you've filed your report," I said. "But it'll have to be early, I have a 10:30 a.m. deadline."

"That's okay," he said. "I check in at 8:00 a.m. and I should have some information for you by that time."

I cleaned up some loose ends on the story. Shot up some film, interviewed some of the neighbors, and left the scene. Going back to my apartment that night the case was bugging me. There were several missing answers; the part about "there was heavy drinking going on at the party"—what did Hansard mean, did this have a hand in Tommy's death? What was the cause of death? How did the body get out in the field? What was the cause of death? How did the party and those at the party hook up with his death? What was he doing prior to the party?

All of these questions I filed in my mind as needing answers tomorrow. I mentally ticked off the contacts I would have to make; the Medical Examiner for cause of death; the police complaint for further details as to motive; a phone call to the parents for their reaction and shock; a check of neighbors for comments on what kind of kid Tommy was; plus others.

I got on the phone early the next morning to Sgt. Hansard. The story would have to be wrapped up early or I would have company looking over my shoulder.

Sgt. Hansard was wise to newspaper deadlines. He reeled off the facts quickly.

"Name's Tommy Furman, F–u–r–m–a–n, fourth letter M as in Mary, sixth letter, N as in Noah. Found in a field near Jasper and Springfield roads. Disappeared from home Friday night. Pulled the old pillow in the bed act. Apparently skipped out after disguising the bed to make it look like he was sleeping in it. His parents did a bed check on him and everything looked all right at the time. The next day he turned up missing and they filed an MP report. Checked with some neighbors and they told me about the teenage party that night at Twin Oaks Ranch. Our preliminary investigation shows that drinking was going on at the party, a lot of it. It's pure speculation right now but he may have been drunk, wandered away from the party, and died of exposure. We'll know better when the lab reports come back."

The story was pretty sketchy, I thought, too many missing parts, particularly on how the body got in the field. Was there foul play?

"Go on Fred," I said, "tell me more."

"There isn't more, it's all speculation at this point. You'll have to wait until we get more facts."

"All right, let's go a different route," I said. "Were there any marks on the body, bruises, like that?"

"Yeah, he had what you might say was a 'fat lip.' He had scratches on his back and—"

"And what?" I asked; sensing an important link was missing.

"Well, his jeans were pulled down beneath his buttocks and his shoes had been taken off and placed near a fence row."

"What significance is that?"

"That's hard to say. The bruises could have happened when he fell on the hard ground. We don't know what to make of the shoes being pulled off, particularly in the wintertime. You'll just have to say 'police are still continuing to investigate.'"

"Horseshit Fred, that's easy for you to say but I've got to have more. This isn't some back page story on the obituary page. It's taking on a lot more importance every time you uncover a new clue. The drinking, the all–night party, the bruises, the jeans being pulled down over the buttocks it all adds up now to page one and my editor will be screaming for more details."

"Christ I've told you everything. You reporters are all the same. You keep coming on for more when there is no more, at least right now."

It was time to soften the blow. I couldn't afford to lose his cooperation at this time. Time to compromise; perhaps work on the warm friend routine.

"Fred," I said. "You and I have been friends for some time. I've never betrayed your trust. Please open up a little more with me. My reputation is at stake."

"Okay, okay," he said. "But remember everything is conjecture at this point and please don't use my name."

I knew what he meant. It was time to bring out the old hackneyed "according to an impeachable source" routine newsmen sometimes use when key sources clam up. It wasn't good reporting but it was effective.

"Okay," I said. "I won't give out names. I'll use the other way."

Fred, too, was wise to the newspaper game. He knew the meaning of 'the other way.'

He paused to reflect, started to say no, then relented.

"Okay, what do you want?"

"Who discovered the body? What happened at the party? Do you have anyone in custody? What was the coroner's ruling on cause of death?"

"We brought out tracking dogs to locate the body but Deputy James Pallard actually found him. We're still checking on the party but we found in the meantime that Tommy had been at another drinking party the night before with other teenagers right in the same neighborhood. On the night of his disappearance there were actually three teenage parties going on at the same time. We don't have anyone in custody but we're checking. There could be some sort of adult negligence involved. The Medical Examiner ruled "death by exposure brought on by ingestion of alcohol." We'll have more when we get the toxicologist's report and the autopsy report."

"That'll get me by for now," I said, "along with what I picked up at the scene."

I didn't tell him but by now I had talked to some of the neighbors by phone, called Tommy's school principal and got general rundown on his background. The story was gaining momentum.

A sense of timing and reporter's instinct prompted me to ask a last question.

"And who is the Toxicologist?" I asked.

It would be worthwhile to follow up.

"Name's Kristen Streeter. She works with Medical Science laboratories in Madison Heights."

I jotted the name down, thinking of an interview later. The time frame was now getting uncomfortable.

At the story planning session that morning my city editor and regional editor had both discussed the case. They had already dummied in space for it. The deadline loomed frantically ahead. An old familiar prickling sensation went up my neck, one I had felt many times before as the clock raced to 10:30.

I slugged in my name and punched away at the computer in short, action sentences.

"A 15 year old Whitfield youth's body was found dead in a field yesterday under mysterious circumstances. The youth, Tommy Furman of Whitfield Township had been dead for 2 1/2 days."

The story continued on with details of the drinking party, the investigation into possible "adult negligence," the Medical Examiner's report, the "unimpeachable sources" information from Hansard and color information I had picked up at the scene and telephone calls later. The headline read: *Teenager Found Dead In Field After Drinking Party.*

At the story planning session the next day I was told to continue on with the case, making further interviews and "keep on top." There were too many underlying circumstances to let the story die after only a one–day exposure. I was told to run my own show."

# Chapter 2

"Hello, I'd like to speak to Kristin Streeter," I said. It was two days later and time for a telephone follow up on the Toxicologist report.

"She'll be with you in a minute," the crisp, businesslike voice said at the other end of the line.

I half mused: "Why do all secretaries have to be so damned cold and efficient. Why can't they answer: 'well, hello, there, honey' in one of those warm, low, sultry voices and then go on to the business at hand? I pondered this and interesting variations of another nature before my daydreams broke up and a voice answered: "Yes, this is Kristin Streeter. Can I help you?"

"Yes, this is Mike Dunn of the *Oakland Herald*. I want to know if you have completed the Toxicologist report on the Tommy Furman case, you know the 15 year old boy who was found in a field near Whitfield?"

"I have," she said, "but I'm not allowed to give it to you over the phone. You may see the report if you wish but I'll need some identification."

The voice was firm and unbending. I saw it was useless to argue. Besides, hadn't my editors given me free reign? There was no other way. I would have to spend some time on a personal interview.

"May I see you tomorrow afternoon, Mrs. Streeter?"

"It's Miss Streeter and yes you may. The report has been completed but not typed. But I can have it for you tomorrow. What time will you be here so I can go over it with you?"

Go over it with me. Lord, I thought, this lady is leaving nothing to chance. One hundred fifty thousand readers of the Herald are not only going to get medical science's version of what happened, but Miss Streeter would make sure the company's image would be preserved and well padded. I made a mental note to look for a Public Relations snow job on the case.

"I'll be there about 2:00 p.m.," I said.

"I'll be ready for you. Goodbye."

Wow, I thought, this lady gets to the point fast and then butts out like a jet turning off its after burner. I wonder if she'll open up. I always had had a bad feeling for people who answered leading questions with straight five word sentences. Interviewing them is like taking out a deeply embedded sliver, a painful process. Sometimes I found in interviewing you get around that by getting them mad—then they really open up on you. But the trick sometimes works in reverse.

I opened the door at Medical Science laboratories the next day and immediately was hit by a pungent smell of chemicals. It reminded me of my old chemistry lab in high school that when some wag got foxy and mixed up a batch of $CS_2$ (Carbon Disulfide). It smelled disgustingly like some one had just broken wind. The odious smell wafted through the halls and study rooms and always there were cries of "oh–oh, someone's done it again." And the culprit, if he were caught, received a stern lecture, but there was always a next time and some one else played out the scenario. One time one of the braver students wore a gas mask in class and he was promptly sent to the Principal for punishment while the class tittered.

"I'm looking for Miss Streeter," I announced. The secretary answered me in that same crisp, business–like voice, "I'll get her, she's doing a test but can breakaway."

My daydreams of Miss Streeter turned out to be 100 percent wrong. She was radiantly beautiful, dark–haired, tall but trim, a bit on the light side but not quite. My keen eye, sharpened by years of practice, detected that she was curvaceous in the right places, had firm white teeth, a natural smile—and a dark tan complexion like she had just spent the past week in Florida. I couldn't tell at a distance whether it was real or patted on. It looked good to me anyhow. She walked stylishly but firmly to an adjoining room and beckoned me to join her. It was the walk of a fashion model, not a toxicologist. She looked ravishingly beautiful in a white lab coat that accentuated her jet–black hair.

This won't be too bad an afternoon, I thought.

My mind began to explore all kinds of interesting situations before we began talking.

I saw myself at the airport where Miss Streeter and I were talking in low voices dripping with emotion. I reached in my pocket, took out two cigarettes, lit one, and handed the other to her. "Listen sweetheart," I said, "You and I may meet in another place, another time, and when we do we can forget all about war, the Nazis, and prejudices. It'll just be you and I together, forever."

With that I walked jauntily to a waiting plane, not looking back once. Her eyes were red with tears as I took off and roared into the darkened cloud filled sky.

My mind jerked back to reality.

"Let's get down to business, Miss Streeter," I said. I put a sneer in my voice, turning my head directly towards her, giving her my best profile. It wasn't a very good performance. Right away she got to the subject.

"About this lab report," she said.

Suddenly my subconscious mind began jabbing me. My conscience prickled with the feeling that something was wrong. Here you are dealing with a terrible tragedy, I thought, and you're daydreaming of a glamorous scene. You're a professional, get off it and go to work.

"On about February 21 did you receive a sample by courier from the Oakland County Medical Examiner's officer relating to the death of Tommy Furman?" I asked.

"Yes I did. We were asked to do a Coma Panel."

The term wasn't familiar to me.

"What is a Coma Panel?"

"It's a title description that stands for comprehensive drug screening which is the panel we offer through Bio Science laboratories. It's a screen that detects about 40 different drugs in serum, urine and gastric juices," she answered matter–of–factly. It was like she was reading from a textbook.

A little buzzer went off in my brain. Newspaper stories, theoretically, are supposed to be aimed at an eighth grade audience. This wasn't. But I went on; I could always write down style, using simpler terms.

"What type of drugs do you analyze?" I asked.

Again the text book delivery.

"We analyze several different drugs; we do therapeutic drug monitoring for anticonvulsants, barbiturates, tranquilizers, alcohol."

"Stop right there. Were you asked to do a Coma Panel on alcohol for Tommy Furman?"

"Yes we did. We received a request to Coma Panel for blood and urine."

"Tell me the results."

"Well, we test the urine for most of the drugs first. The concentration of substances in the urine is generally higher than it is in the blood. We will usually detect something in the urine before we will find it in the blood. We do a volatile analysis. We inject the specimen directly into a Gas Chromotrophy instrument and look for the presence of ethanol, methanol, isopropanol, or Acetone. They are volatile substances."

"And is ethanol related to alcohol or in eight grade jargon, booze?"

"Yes, ethanol is the colorless liquid in wine, beer, whisky, gin and other fermented and distilled liquors that makes them intoxicating."

Again the text book style. Did this woman ever become human?

"Well, did you get a reading from your tests? How much alcohol was in the system?"

"We do not quantitate alcohol in urine," she said. "We don't feel that you can get an accurate quantitatum of the alcohol."

I wondered what book she got that out of.

"Well, then, what was the blood alcohol percentage that you got from the blood sample?" I asked.

"About .074."

"And was Tommy drunk under this percentage?"

"That's something only the courts can decide. It depends on a lot of things; how much greasy food was in the body, the physical condition of the person, much more than I can say. And, too, the body metabolizes or dissipates the alcohol at a given rate. That goes right on to death. At the time of death the percentage could have been much higher, even to the state of being comatose or semi–comatose."

"Did you test for anything else, like so–called street drugs?"

"We do not test for street drugs, like Marijuana, LSD, or Mescaline or Heroin. Such drugs would be found upon analysis of the bile or gastric juices and not be evidenced by the blood/urine."

Somehow I had lost an important piece of information along the way and I wasn't happy. Maybe Tommy wasn't high on alcohol at all. Maybe he wasn't drunk and perhaps his death was drug oriented. This lady wasn't about to tell me. In fact, gathering from her answers, maybe she couldn't tell me. I pressed doggedly on, bulldog style.

"All right," I said in half anger. "Just what DO you test for in this laboratory?" I looked around me at the machines, the test tubes and swept my hand in disbelief.

This time she was the one who was angry.

"MISTER Dunn," she said, eyes flashing. "I have been a medical technologist for 14 years. My credentials are flawless. When I do a test I do it for evidence of…."

And here she paused briefly before drawing up to her haughtiest, straight–laced position: "Opiates, Codeine, Morphine, Phencyclidine, Demerol, Benze Diazepines which include Valium, Librium and their Metabolites. I test for Salicylates, Acetamino-phen, the volatiles as I said, Methanol, Ethanol, Isopropanol and

Acetone, Amphetamines, Methamphetamines, Cocaine, Ben-zeleogonines, Efedrom, Phenyl–Proponel, Methaqualone, Darvon, and its Metabolite Nor Darvon."

Her dissertation complete, Miss Streeter looked me straight in the eyes and queried "anything else you want to know MISTER Dunn?"

This time it was my time to squirm.

"No thank you, you have been most complete."

I broke off, properly squelched and humiliated.

On an after thought I managed a final question, hoping that she wasn't too ticked off to answer it.

"In the things that you mentioned did you find any other material and after testing for ethanol or ethyl alcohol, what were the results of the tests for all the other substances that you men-tioned, I mean, leaving out street drugs?"

"There was nothing detected of other chemical substances."

"So Tommy wasn't high on drugs that night he died?"

"I didn't say that. You would have to test the bile for gastric juices and this kind of information."

"And where would I find out about this?"

"I believe these samples might have been sent to a laboratory in California."

So much for that theory the results would have to wait on California.

There wasn't much more to talk about. I filed that lovely face and its gorgeous body in my memory bank and decided to leave.

"One more thing," I added. "I'm sorry for the outburst, I'm running into so many detours on this case it's making me wonder if I'll ever get to the bottom of it. Please forgive me."

She softened immediately and said quietly, "that's all right, I understand. It's a very emotional case; a young boy found laying dead in a field of unknown causes."

It was a sympathetic statement and I wasn't about to let it sit there.

"Perhaps we can discuss more of this over dinner. I mean some of the parts that are missing."

I lied on that. I had all that I needed at this point but I had to see her again.

She took the lead, thankfully.

"Yes that would be okay with me but I'm limited on what I can and am authorized to release by Medical Science laboratories. My job is at stake, you know and my profession."

I scrambled for my address book, carefully wrote down her telephone and address, and promised to call. You can bet that was one promise I intended to keep.

The day had been long and hard. Problems and questions kept pestering my mind. It was time for "twofers" at the Whitside Hotel.

# Chapter 3

The Whitside Hotel is an old three–story brick hotel with a storied history dating back to the 1800's.

In its day it was the social gathering place of the town. One of the oldest social clubs in the nation had its beginning there. It was called the George Washington Club and was started in the late 1800's by a patriarch of the community who wished to perpetuate the memory of George Washington.

A speaker who wished to outdo his predecessor in extolling the virtues of old George always marked its meetings.

Sometimes the remarks weren't all on the up side of George.

A tryst under a Maple tree with George and a curvaceous widow of the colonial times once shocked the assemblage and the speaker, who had intended to inject something lively into the staid proceedings was never asked back.

Then the meetings once again got back to tradition, the perseverance of Colonial times, Martha Washington importing ice cream from France to the dinner tables of America, and of course the endless anecdotes about George and the Cherry tree and the others.

In its time the annual George Washington Club meetings were the top social event of the season. Ladies in attendance wore wide, feathery hats, long armed white gloves, and wired petticoats. Thimble bowls gave you a chance to daintily dip your fingers in water before the next course was served and only the finest lace was used for the tablecloths.

Now the conservative old hotel had shifted its gears and was a gourmet–dining restaurant. Its walls were lined with old time pictures of Whitside in its lumbering and railroad days and one room was converted into a simulated Pullman car.

The main floor was pretty much a gourmet restaurant, but, ah, the basement was made into the format of an old fashioned saloon.

It was here that I was headed.

I had good reason to. Not only was the atmosphere less heady but the drinks were considerably cheaper. You could saunter into the saloon with blue jeans and a sloppy T–shirt. Upstairs, it was strictly jackets and cocktail dresses. As I sat on an old fashioned bar stool, a bartender with a checkered vest and sleeves held up by arm garters asked me what I would have.

My vision blurred and I saw myself in spurs, cowboy boots, and a high cowboy hat. I looked over at the entranceway and it became a pair of swinging doors.

"Whisky—and put the bottle down right here," I thought. But it's not what I said.

"Yeah, give me a rum and coke." The bartender sat down two drinks in front of me. My mind shocked back into reality.

It was the policy of the hotel to have a band on Friday and Saturday nights. I looked around the room. A three–piece band was at it and four or five couples were out on the floor. The band was playing a mixture of 50's and late 40's music. The crowd showed its age as the floor filled up alternately with a combination of seniors and couples in their late 40's. The scenario was not only comfortable and danceable but it was profitable.

The band launched into a moderate rock version of "Heart Break Hotel" with Elvis Presley type vocalist handling the lyrics followed by a smooth, mellow blend of "Star Dust" and "Very Thought of You."

Somehow, in the strange pattern of life, I had never taken to the modern trends of music. Perhaps it was the influence of my late father who had at one time been a semi professional musician (as well as a newspaperman) and refused to accept loud music and the advent of "Rock."

Strangely, I followed his thinking, in spite of peer pressure to accept rock and roll and the rest of the modern day music. As a cornet player in high school my fellow band members had thought me "weird." I was always following the big bands and their music. I loved the music—and the sound. Apparently I wasn't alone. One time I went to a nearby ballroom to hear Tex Beneke's band and I was startled to see a young couple in their twenties dancing Jitterbug. When the dance ended I was curious enough to ask them why.

They had a simple reason.

"We love music of the 40's and we're studying Jitterbug," they said. They had been dancing this way and listening to the big bands for two years, even taking classes in Jitterbug. I felt even better when Tex suggested that the young men and women of today are going back to the "Big Band Sound." Somehow my life took on more balance that night.

One of the dangers of "twofers" is friends. Ordinarily the thought of shelling out dough for two drinks at a time would warp young conservative minds. But two for the price of one! What a difference! A chance for a reputation as "The Big Spender."

One twofer followed another as friends scrambled to outdo themselves. Money was carelessly tossed on the bar, not even counted when picked up.

I found myself somewhat heady; the music, the smoke, and the beat of the drums were getting to me. As the band launched into "One o'clock jump" I couldn't help myself. My feet led me to the small stage fronting the band and I was tapping my feet, rolling my head and snapping my fingers.

"Hey, Mike, want to join us?"

It was 'Moose,' my buddy in football playing days.

"Why not?" I said.

The cornet player had already shoved his horn at me. My eyes sparked as I took off his mouthpiece and inserted my own from my pocket.

I always carry a substitute mouthpiece with me wherever I go. Frequently, when I'm bored I take it out and blow a few "hot lips."

The band picked up its tempo and soon I was swinging to "Sweet Georgia Brown."

The mood had never been better. The licks were hot and sweet. The high notes were never crisper. Life was good. Old Scoop Dunn was ridin' high.

I had knocked the Furman case to another world, another dimension.

The streetlights of Whitside looked blurry and fuzzy that night as I slouched out the door. I opened the windows of the Mustang as far down as they would go and eased off the throttle. A cold February wind blasting through the windows helped me to get safely to my apartment.

I slept soundly and happily.

# Chapter 4

Having Sunday to rest up my mind was sharp and clean on Monday at the Herald.

My lead went like this: "A Madison Heights Toxicologist said today that Tommy Furman, the 15 year old Whitfield youth found dead of exposure in a field after a teenage party was not on drugs."

I suddenly cut short. It's not what she said, not at all, I thought.

She said he was not on Opium, Valium, Librium, and 30 other substances. (I winced when I recalled her name jangling on the subject). She could not tell me about so–called "Street Drugs," Marijuana, LSD, or Heroin. That would have to wait the California results.

I realized then that I couldn't really write anything on the drug angle until I had more facts, which up to now were skimpy. It was time for the follow–up on "Charla." The thought shattered me. "No, not that." The Furman case was out for today's paper needed more clarification. I could still pick up parts of the interview, however, other parts would have to wait on the California tests, perhaps a talk with the Medical Examiner and further reports from the Sheriff's Department.

I crushed the copy paper and in anger tossed it into the wastebasket. It was a disappointing day. I felt I had let the Herald and myself down. But I was determined to make it up later.

# Chapter 5

One of my day by day assignment checks is the Prosecuting Attorney's Office.

My check there today I knew would be more than routine. I had heard they had established motives and were ready to issue warrants in the Furman case. My good buddy Sgt. Hansard had just briefed me on that.

The receptionist greeted me with a smile and a hands–on–hip flippant remark of "What's the latest scoop on the Herald today—what skullduggery is going on in the Mayor's office and who's the latest rape victim?"

It was a typical of the airy greetings a newsman gets on his rounds. A reporter has a hard time living down the old cliché label of "scoop," a holdover of the old 'Hold the Press for Replate' tag.

I shot back something like 'no comment at this time there will be a press conference later', hoping the light remark would tie in with her old shoe routine.

It didn't. She didn't think the answer was too funny. I changed the subject.

"Who's taking over the Furman case?" I asked.

"William Pillister, assistant prosecuting attorney."

I had known Pillister for a couple of months. He was one of the "Young Lions" of the Prosecutor's office. He was not the best trial lawyer on the staff, that is, he was not gifted with words, nor glib or suave with the smart comebacks, but he was dedicated and very thorough on research. When he got through with a case it was like a package all neatly tied up and ready for mailing. Nothing was left to chance. He was a young, easy going man with a jet black beard and hair cut in the contemporary style, just long enough to look stylish and short enough to earn the respect of his elders.

I asked the secretary to buzz him. In a couple of minutes he came out and ushered me into a neat little office crammed with law books and an uninspiring metal grey desk.

"I'm busy and you're busy so let's get down to business," I began. This would be a no–nonsense talk, full of detail and important facts. I know that from past dealings with Pillister. "I hear you've issued warrants in the Furman case." I said.

"Yes, we're charging both men involved in the party and drinking with Involuntary Manslaughter."

"Give me the details."

"Our investigation has turned up that Robert S. Conley, 46, of Whitfield Township and James W. Hunter, 43, same township, are we feel, guilty of adult negligence in the death of Tommy Furman. Conley is charged with furnishing Tommy and a companion with a pint of Southern Comfort liquor. It was at Hunter's house where a teenage drinking party was taking place the night that Tommy died. We believe he wondered away from the party in an intoxicated condition, passed out in an adjacent field and died of Hypothermia brought on by exposure and inability to take care of himself in his intoxicated element." I might add that Involuntary Manslaughter in a situation such as this is a Landmark case. It is an attempt on our part to make adults more responsible at teenage parties."

"What do you mean a Landmark case?"

"Well, in most instances, adults caught in a situation such as this are charged with Contributing to the Delinquency of a Minor, a misdemeanor with a maximum sentence of only 90 days, this in spite of negligence causing death. On the other hand the maximum sentence for Involuntary Manslaughter is 15 years. We believe it is time to call a halt to irresponsible actions at these parties which we know are going on every weekend in the county."

"How do you know these parties are that widespread?"

"Look, the night Tommy died there were three teenage drinking parties going on right in the area. Only the night before another party took place, which Tommy attended. In our questioning of teenagers at one of the parties we found out that one of the girls had been drinking heavily since she was 12 years old. Go to any community; ask any local law officer, they'll all tell you the same story. At graduation time it's absolutely horrible the amount of drinking going on."

"If this is so widespread," I said, "how come more cases haven't been tried on Manslaughter instead of "Contributing"— aren't you guys interested in cutting down the carnage?"

"There's a story that goes with that. I put this case into the computer and could only find two cases in the entire country where Manslaughter was charged. One was out west, the other in the Midwest. In both cases they were either dismissed or the charges watered down."

"Why is that?"

"I have some ideas on that. In the first place if the case goes to jury, most juries, strange to say, are sympathetic to the defendant. That's because a number of them have been in the same boat. Most adults, at some time, have hosted teenage parties where drinking has been going on. Some have been responsible but most have not. Dad remembers back to the time that he was on the other side of the fence when he didn't want to give the kids the image that he was an old grouch. He gave in to the drinking, even had a few belts to go along with them. Because the cases were dismissed naturally there is no file to draw on for substantiation. Secondly," he continued, "Manslaughter is one of the vaguest charges to back up. Even judges can't agree on its definition. In the case of Hunter we have to prove that he knowingly and wantonly disregarded his duties as a parent to responsibly patrol the party at his house and in the case of Conley we have to prove that he knew the disastrous results of furnishing minors with 100 proof Southern Comfort. A conviction in this case would greatly clarify the law regarding responsibility. And that's why it is a landmark case. This country needs to make it clear that a person is criminally liable for negligent acts leading to the death or serious injury of a young teenager."

The story was off to a good start, starting to round out. Not only did it have interesting reading—it was now starting to take on a new, strong, moral lesson. I pressed on.

"How many teenagers were at this party and was alcohol the only substance consumed?"

"We talked to some young persons at the party and they said some Marijuana smoking was going on outside. Reportedly a white Pontiac Grand Prix drove up in the middle of the party and offered Mescaline but we don't have hard evidence on that. There were 20 to 25 persons at the party, according to our investigation."

"Was Tommy high on Marijuana?"

"We don't have evidence to substantiate that. Some kids said he had a couple of puffs on a joint that was being passed around but evidently not enough to get high on."

I finished the interview with a few more questions, went back to the newspaper to finish out the story with facts about events leading up to the party, description of the body when found, amount of alcohol found in the body, background on the two men charged and time of their examination, slugged in my name and set the headline.

The next day the Herald highlighted Pillister's story on the front page. My comments on the responsibility of adults drew bold face type; the rest of the article was in lightface.

Even my cranky, hard–nosed editor was pleased.

"Stay on with the story," he said, "pick it up as it goes and feed it to us, along with your other assignments. This is good stuff and we could stand some more circulation in this area."

A few days later I got a call from Mrs. Furman. She had read the article and was anxious to discuss it with me. She sounded like she wished to cooperate. I had a feeling she wanted publicity to help other young men avoid what had happened to Tommy. It was worth a follow up and I could get some comments and color stuff prior to the examination. We made an appointment for the next day at her house.

Once again the Mustang and I were on our way northward towards Whitfield. I pulled into the gravel driveway of the Furman house and looked up at a neat, white two story dwelling, a look alike to hundreds of such dwellings that dot the Michigan rural countryside.

I rang the bell and an attractive, trim woman in her late 30's ushered me into the living room. She offered me cookies and coffee. She made me comfortable to the point of embarrassment. I hated to get to a subject that I knew would be very painful to her. Her hands clasped and unclasped.

As we sat down the flickering light of an old fashioned wood stove painted strange figures and symbols on the plastered walls. The setting seemed right out of Currier and Ives.

"I'm so glad you came," she began. "I had to talk to someone about my son. I know I can't bring him back but perhaps I can help others to avoid what happened to my Tommy, through your newspaper."

Her eyes glistened as she talked and she fought back the tears that came quickly, then stopped. I couldn't help notice the inner strength that eventually helped her win her battle for composure. To calm her I quickly got to the subject, painful as it was. Talking about it, I thought, will help simmer her down.

"Tell me, Mrs. Furman, what kind of boy was Tommy?" I asked. "Did you have any trouble controlling him?"

Once again the eyes moistened, but this time only for a second.

"Not readily," she said. "Once he fought one day and he skipped one day, but nothing really bad, no. Maybe he was a little bit rebellious but all teenagers are like that. You see Tommy is my son by my first marriage. My husband and I lived near Detroit at the time and after my second marriage we moved out here. I think Tommy was changing for the better in his new environment. He wanted to be on the tennis team. He was struggling for recognition."

"Did Tommy do much drinking?"

This time there was a flicker in the eyes. It passed quickly.

"Some, but not a lot. As I say he was coming around, getting more confidence in himself, opening up more to me and my second husband."

"Was he at a party the night before the Conley party?"

"Yes he was, but he was not drunk. He had strict orders not to do that and we picked him up early in the evening. My husband even smelled his breath to make sure that he had not been drinking. The next night we had dinner and then my husband and I sat around and watched TV with Tommy. Then he excused himself about 10:45 p.m. My last conversation with him was about a girl named Gail. He wanted to know how old she was. I told him and he kissed me goodnight and went downstairs to bed."

"Did you check on Tommy before you and your husband went to bed that night?"

"Yes we did, I mean he did. He looked in on him about midnight. It looked like Tommy was sleeping but when we awoke in the morning and didn't see him for breakfast we knew something was wrong. That was when my husband found the pillows made up to look like he was sleeping. We then called neighbors around to find out if they had seen him and then we called police. They say when they found Tommy he was wearing only a T-shirt, denim vest, and tennis shoes. I heard that he was thrown out of the party and locked out in the freezing weather because he had been vomiting and they didn't want him to throw up inside the house. How can anyone be that cruel? Is that true, Mr. Dunn?"

I told her I had been told the same thing but only as hearsay. If it were true, however, I thought, it would be important to point out the thoughtlessness and indifference that could have resulted in Tommy's death. In the back of my mind I was determined to keep this alive, callousness, irresponsibility, adult negligence. The publicity could help teach a lesson.

In a pensive thought she continued: "A lot of my son's friends have changed their habits and quit drinking, gone on the wagon because of this. I hope there is a conviction on these two men because I wouldn't want them to go back to drinking again and know that no one is to blame. I hope you print that my Tommy was not a heavy drinker or drug user. There has been a lot of talk that he was. My other two children, 14 and 12, have been very distraught over the events and the things they are saying about Tommy at school. I just can't get it out of my head that there was only one adult at that party."

She was fumbling for words now; it was difficult for her to express herself. The painful moments were starting to get to her. The interview had reached the awkward stage. With her comments and my background information I had enough for now, anyhow. I asked a few more routine questions and readied to leave. I thanked her and left. I wanted to see Sgt. Hansard on my way home. He had told me that he had interviewed several of the teenagers at the party and I was anxious to read the reports.

# Chapter 6

Sgt. Hansard wasn't in his office but he had left word that I could look over the reports. The bulging case file stared at me. I was anxious to get to work. Never had I been so intrigued by a subject, tragic as it was. I started reading.

INTERVIEW WITH CAROLE LANSING—
RE: THOMAS FURMAN CASE

"Would you please give your name?"

"Carole Lansing."

"Did your daughter want you to help throw a party for her boyfriend, Max Conley, at Twin Oaks Ranch the night of February 21, 1981?"

"Yes she did. She asked me if I would help her get the booze or a keg."

"What did you say to that?"

"I told her I wouldn't help her. I wouldn't get the booze and keg."

"In spite of that did she later pick up the liquor?"

"Yes, she was with an adult who purchased it with her money and turned it over to her. She told me that she had originally intended to buy it from a friend who was a bartender but that got all messed up because the bar had been investigated earlier on a liquor violation."

"Where did she get the money for this purchase?"

"From her savings account."

"Are you acquainted with Robert S. Conley?"

"Yes—I live with him."

"Do you know Tommy Furman?"

"Yes, he is a friend of my daughters."

"Tell me, in your own words, what happened on February 21, 1981, in connection with Tommy Furman and a teenage party at Twin Oaks Ranch."

"Well, Bob and I were in his trailer just visiting and my daughter asked me if I would get her some booze for her boyfriend, Max. He was having a birthday and she wanted to throw a party for him. I told her I wouldn't have anything to do with that. She pleaded with Bob to help her, saying that he shouldn't be such an old fogie and he reluctantly agreed to help her out. They went to a liquor store in Grand Blanc and I understand Bob purchased some liquor and beer for her. They put the stuff in the trunk and came home. She knew that Tommy was going to be at the party so she had Bob buy her a pint of Southern Comfort for him cause he likes it. That's all I know."

END OF INTERVIEW

\* \* \*

INTERVIEW WITH GERALD L. SOMMERS, MARCH 20, 1981

"What is your name?"

"Gerald L. Sommers."

"Were you at a party at Twin Oaks Ranch on February 21, 1981?"

"Yes, I was."

"How would you describe the condition of Tommy Furman the night of the party?"

"Wasted."

"What do you mean, wasted?"

"He was staggering all over, drunk."

"When did you come into contact with Tommy?"

"In the bathroom. He was lying on the floor. It looked like he was going to get sick. I asked Mike Bettsler if he would give me a hand and we took him outside and laid him on the ground. He was getting up and that's why us kids locked the door—so he wouldn't come back in and get sick in the house. I heard someone say 'don't let him have any more to drink, or something like that.'"

"Did he have any cuts or bruises on him at that time?"

"No sir."

"Did you hear that Mike Dooley had beaten him up in a fight and that he had been dumped into a pick up truck?"

"I heard that. It must have happened later. I guess Tommy came to and someone let him back into the house. It must have been when he came back in that he got into the fight."

"Who furnished the booze and beer for the party?"

"Well, a lot of kids brought their own. Mr. Hunter furnished a six pack and then it was all gone and he went out and bought a 12 pack about midnight."

"When you took Tommy outside did he have any physical signs to indicate someone had smashed him in the mouth? In other words did he have a 'fat lip?'"

"No sir, he didn't."

"Did he resist you in any way when you took him outside from the bathroom?"

"No sir, he didn't."

"Did you in moving him have any occasion to scratch part of his arm or inflict any type of bruise on his body?"

"No sir."

"When you put him down on the ground did you immediately, as they say in your language 'do a 180,' walk back into the house and leave him there?"

"Yes we did."

"What happened then?"

"We went back to get Tommy later and he wasn't there."

"What was Mr. Hunter doing all this time?"

"Well, when we found Tommy lying in the bathroom he asked who was going to take him home. Shelly Comstock said she and her boyfriend would, after he had sobered up a little."

"Have you ever seen Tommy take any drugs?"

"Well, outside we were all dragging on a joint and Tommy had two or three hits on it, along with the rest of us. He's taken Mescaline before that I know of. I hadn't seen him take it but he said he had. He's taken drugs, I understand, but he ain't no fiend, you know what I mean. He used it sometimes but so does everybody else around our neighborhood."

"Do you take drugs?"

"A lot of us people do, it's common."

"What do you mean by 'people'?"

"People. I mean like my family, my brother and kids down the street and stuff."

"And there were 'people' going in and out of the party all evening to take 'tokes on joints'?"

"No, there was one guy outside with it. I think he had two joints and they were being passed around."

"What response came from Tommy after you took him outside?"

"He sort of rolled over and moaned, like he was sick or something."

"Did you see him after that?"

"Yeah, I saw him later out by the manure spreader. He was sort of talking to himself. He asked for more beer. I saw him fall in the barn by the manure spreader. He fell into a trench a couple of times and staggered around. He was mumbling most of the time."

"Who was he mumbling to?"

"That's the funny thing. He didn't seem to be talking to anyone. It was almost like he was talking to the cows. I heard some people say we should take him home but nothing was done about it."

END OF INTERVIEW

\* \* \*

INTERVIEW OF DENISE PURVIS, MARCH 22, 1981

"What is your name?"

"Denise Purvis."

"Were you at the party at Twin Oaks Ranch on February 21, 1981?"

"Yes I was."

"Did you observe the condition of James Hunter at this party?"

"Yes I did. He was cold sober."

"Did you see Tommy Furman at the party?"

"Yes I did."

"Where was he when you saw him?"

"He was laying in the mud, not making any sounds at all."

"Did he ask you or anyone to help him up or anything like that?"

"Yeah, he asked Mike Bremer to pick him up."

"When did you arrive at the party?"

"About 7:30 p.m."

"When did you start drinking?"

"When the beer got there."

"Did you stop drinking at any time?"

"Yeah, when the beer ran out."

"How much beer did Tommy Furman consume?"

"I would guess about seven beers."

"Was Mr. Hunter mingling in the party with the guests or was he keeping more or less to himself?"

"He was keeping more or less to his own business. He was watching TV in a bedroom."

"Did he bring in any beer to the party?"

"Yeah, probably about 2 1/2 cases."

"During the course of the party did many people go in and out of the house to smoke pot? Was this some sort of rule that was laid down that no one would smoke pot inside the house?"

"Yeah, it was okay to drink beer inside but the hard stuff we hit outside. It was sort of a gentleman's agreement."

"At one point did a white Grand Prix pull up to the house and someone make an inquiry as to whether or not anyone wanted to buy Mescaline?"

"Yes."

"Do you drink frequently? Please be honest about it."

"Yeah."

"You were at the Robert Packer house party the night before were you not, and that was a 'kegger'?"

"Yeah."

"How many cups of beer did you have at that party?"

"I don't remember."

"Is that because you were smashed?"

"Yeah."

"How many drinks do you think you had?"

"Somebody was making a joke about that, they said I drank 21."

"How often would you 'party down'?"

"Every other weekend there would be a party somewhere, sometimes two or three."

"How old are you?"

"14 years old."

"How long have you been drinking?"

"I dunno, maybe a year and a half."

"So you started at some time when you were like 12 1/2?"

"No, 13."

END OF INTERVIEW

The next day a headline in the Herald blared:

*"Teenagers recall events at drinking party."*

The story raised a lot of talk in the area. It was obvious many people didn't know the extent of teenage drinking parties going on right in their midst. I was satisfied that the issue was coming to a head. My editor told me the paper was getting a lot of comments on the articles and to stay with it.

Shortly after the story appeared I had a telephone call from someone at the party who was real upset with the story. The unidentified voice said I was terribly wrong on my remarks about Hunter not mingling with the guests and making checks. They said we should print a retraction. Before I could ask who it was they hung up. The conversation would bear checking out.

My mind was fogged with rumors and pieces of evidence that didn't fit.

It was time for a "Break." My social calendar had been neglected too long while my mind grappled with story problems. It was like one big pathway suddenly merging into a dozen little ones. It was all too confusing. I decided to do something about it.

A mental picture came into my mind of a certain tall, trim, toxicologist who bristled with wise cracks when she got mad and who could use a lesson in relaxation, maybe over a mixed drink or two and soft music in the background.

I dialed her number.

The friendly "hello" that followed brought into focus a familiar face with crinkly eyes, a natural friendly smile and a million–dollar figure. The electricity started to flow.

"Hi, it's me again, Mike Dunn, you know the guy who stirred you up the other day and then apologized."

"Yes, I recognize your voice—it's nice of you to call."

This time there was no primness, no artificiality, no crispness, and no business talk.

Could this woman actually be two people? I had heard of this kind of person, crisp, and business like at their profession, a real relaxed, friendly person outside of it.

I couldn't find anything wrong with the thought. After all, leave out all the cordialities, the small talk, the endless banter of clichés, one less meaningful than the other and what have you got? Sensibility that's what. And why not? I warmed up to the idea. Everyone could use some of this. Like myself, I was always spending useless time getting to the point. Why not get quickly to the meat and potatoes so you can enjoy the dessert?

"I'm right in the middle of the Furman case," I said, "you know the 15 year old boy mixed up on the party at Twin Oaks. Everything is out of focus, the case is getting to me, and I'm game for a cocktail and dinner. How about you?"

"Well, what time frame are you talking about?"

"Tonight."

"You must think I must be pretty socially backward to call and expect me to go out on a date the same night you ask."

Damn it, I thought, there goes that bristleness again.

What do I have to do to break down that set–in–stone mask? Maybe I should retrench a bit. Maybe more of a platonic build up.

I softened my tone, smiled, and in my best "telephone language" imagined giving her a friendly pat on the cheek.

"I'm not really trying to put a "make" on you. I want to know you better; I like your personality. I think you're outgoing, and so am I. I think we could exchange some pleasantries, look at the world from different viewpoints, so to speak."

Her reaction seemed to soften. In my mind I pictured her features relaxing. I could see this was the best approach.

"I think I would like that," she said.

I added: "It's been a long day for the both of us, perhaps a little relaxation would be good for both of us."

"Yes, I agree."

The voice was actually friendly, vibrant.

"Where are we going?" she asked.

"I'll tell you when I get there. Don't you like mysteries?"

"Only, if there's nothing ugly and horrendous at the end."

"There's nothing ugly or horrendous at the end."

I visualized her face again. This time it was soft and smiling. Instead of the lab coat I saw a bulky, turtle neck sweater, a trim pair of slacks and long legs sprawled on a davenport. I saw soft, long, black hair, with a hand pulling absently on a snarl and satin pink slippers crossed elegantly. My mind wondered happily, enticingly.

Back to reality I said: "I'll pick you up in an hour and a half—at your place. But I don't have your address, just your phone number."

"It's 12368 Parkside in Rochester. I live in one of those apartment complexes."

The Mustang seemed perkier and smoother as I headed towards Rochester. Perhaps it, too, had a premonition of something in the air.

I always like to think of my cars in terms of being human.

When I speak of having an exhaust system removed I whimsically see an operating table with a car on it, with a front end like a face. A surgeon has taken a scalpel and miraculously the metal has become skin. He cuts away and takes out a long, rusty muffler. He carelessly throws it into a metal container with one of those foot–operated covers and it clanks loudly as it hits bottom. Another surgeon with plastic gloves lifts a new muffler from a sterile, windowed refrigerator and moves over to the first surgeon.

He carefully hands it to the surgeon. The nurse wipes the sweat from the surgeon's forehead and the muffler is neatly inserted, the outside skin sutured and low and behold the little car is put on the floor, accelerates, and runs out the door.

Like every car buff I had a name for my car. I called her "Mert." Mert had bad kidneys, was forever using oil, but she always faithfully delivered me safely home, no matter my condition.

Like most pretty girls Mert was sometimes good and sometimes bad. And when she was bad she was really bad. I mean, like a cracked cylinder head, a busted water pump, or a cracked distributor head. As an amateur mechanic I frequently fixed her myself and I found myself doing more of this because I couldn't bear the thought of parting with dear old "Mert."

At Kris's apartment I rang the doorbell and waited to see whether my imagined vision matched its real counterpart.

I wasn't disappointed.

Kris ushered me into the apartment. She didn't walk to the davenport; she flowed to it like a midnight cordial flows down your throat, warm and honey–like.

"Would you like a drink?" she asked.

"Never turn down the first drink of the day." I said, trying desperately to appear light and funny, even though I didn't exactly feel the part. I hate clichés but here I was into my first and the evening had just started.

"What will you have?" she asked.

"A Martini. Do you know how to make one?" I said.

"I'm not sure I can satisfy you with my version. I hear Martini drinkers are awfully particular. Perhaps you would like to mix your own. How do you like yours?"

"I guess you might call me a 90 percenter. I vaporize it with the cork from a Vermouth bottle. The rest is gin."

"That sounds pretty powerful."

"I don't have too many, that's the secret, one and out."

"Will you mix me one, too?"

"The 90 percenter version?"

"I'll try just one."

We sat and drank slowly, exchanging tidbits of conversation about her work and my work.

I asked and found out about her past life. She had not always been a toxicologist. At one time she worked in fashion wear at an area shopping mall. Nothing like Nieman–Marcus, she assured me, but close.

She had some interesting stories to tell.

Like the time her department put on a "Men's Only" party near Christmas time to entice men to buy Christmas gifts for "their ladies." There was plenty of booze on hand and high–class fashion models were recruited from Detroit to add to the frivolity. The more booze the men drank the more liberal they became with their wallets. Some of the lingerie the models displayed resulted in a pat or two on the behind but the models were well paid for that. At the end the owners were smiling as they added up the night's receipts.

However, some of the sizes didn't fit too well because when the men who had imbibed a bit too much, were asked about that, they replied "The size you're wearing will fit just fine."

Unfortunately, the models were slim and tall and the men's "ladies" were short and fat.

After Christmas there was a long parade of distraught wives or sweethearts bringing back the undersized fashion wear.

But, she said, most of the women took it in stride and actually walked out of the store with more merchandise than the men had bought, thanks to credit cards and the women knowing that their men would like to avoid embarrassment.

I chimed in with my favorite news–story about a young felon who escaped into the woods after his crime and was chased by bloodhounds by the sheriff's department. It was front–page stuff and of course I embellished it a bit by bringing in the baying of the hounds, the felon tripping and falling and getting scratched by the underbrush.

The guy was apprehended and ended up in jail until his arraignment. He was able to get out on bond and showed up at the newspaper office shortly afterwards.

I saw him come in the door. He had long hair, torn blue jeans, long angular face, and weird piercing eyes, plus a dark beard.

I was a little apprehensive as he said to me: "I want to talk to the guy who wrote the story about me fleeing into the woods with the bloodhounds chasing me."

He looked menacing and I wondered if he was toting a gun or knife in those faded blue jeans.

But, having faced up to the other stories where I was the culprit, I ventured: "I guess I'll have to own up to that—was there something wrong with the story?"

"Not a bit," he said. "I really like it. I would like to buy a dozen more copies, three or four to my mom and dad, some to my brothers, cousins and nephews."

I gave him the papers, didn't charge him a nickel, and ushered him out the door.

"I've seen everything," I said to myself.

But now an hour had passed like a speeding train going through a tunnel. If we were going to dinner, like I had planned, it was time to break.

"Shall we leave?" I asked. It was one of those pauses that give people a chance to bring the conversation back to reality.

"Where are we going?"

"I have dinner reservations at the Whitside Hotel. It's only 30 minutes from here. You'll love the place, it's old, it's unique and it's charming."

I didn't add that it was expensive. But this was an evening I wanted to file and bring up as a mental tape recording of pleasant moments. Money was nothing. I repeated the sentence "money is nothing." Somehow it didn't sound so good the second time around.

At the hotel a gracious hostess dressed in a Martha Washington costume with long plaid dress and perky little white hat escorted us to a table next to a large picture of "Booster's Day" in old time Whitfield. Instead of cars there were horse carriages of all types and there appeared to be some kind of activity going on in the middle of the street, perhaps a hog calling contest.

Candlelight and a glass of wine set the stage for conversation that was light and on the airy side until somehow we got around to the Furman case which up to this time had been only on the edge of our thoughts, like a car moving towards a deep cliff, only to stop at the brink.

"I can't get over all the side roads this case is taking," I said. The remark was half–light, half heavy. By now the case was constantly in my thoughts. It was impossible to discard it—it even permeated candlelight and wine. I hadn't intended to bring it up but here it was. She didn't try to cast it off. She seemed interested and I was glad. It was our secret conversation piece. It was a spiritual bond between us.

"What do you mean?" she asked, her eyes showing interest.

"Like who's to blame for the whole thing?"

"Explain."

"I mean there was the kids who took him outside and placed him on the driveway in freezing temperatures, then locked the door so he couldn't come back in and get ill. And there's this guy outside with Marijuana, passing it around to the kids. Isn't he to blame too? And why did they take him outside anyhow? If they had left him inside they could have at least put him in the basement; he would have slept it off and been no worse off for the experience."

"Yes," she said, "but you have to deal in priorities. Someone organized the party, someone bought the booze, and someone hosted the party. They are the main ones to blame."

I'm glad that I know this lady, I thought. She has the knack of sifting thought the worthless and getting to the worthwhile. The biggest job in establishing responsibility in the end will go like she says. We discussed other aspects of the case; she was wonderfully patient as I vented my frustrations on her.

I told her I was looking for more angles; there were many missing parts to be explored. The scientific angle interested me because I had a feeling some of the missing links were tied to blood/alcohol evidence and biological studies.

"I know I haven't been that helpful to you, Mike," she said "but perhaps there is someone in my field who can. After all we were only given samples to lab test. Why don't you try the Medical Examiner's office? I don't know that much about him but I'm sure his office has pertinent information.

Our conversation dwindled into niceties and small talk. The hour was getting late. It had been a stimulating, interesting evening.

The ride home that night in the Mustang was unbelievably thrilling and exciting. A full moon lit the cold, black sky. The drinks, the conversation, and the gourmet meal had done its part. My pocketbook was empty but my heart was full. The warm, strong kiss in parting stirred my blood and I walked briskly to "Mert" thinking all the way that the evening had held a thousand delights. It was teenage glow all over again.

# Chapter 7

I'm not much on death. I have a theory about it. If thoughts of death depress me I go somewhere the opposite is operating in full glow—life. It works every time. But this time death was uppermost in my mind and I had no choice but to face it.

I drove Mert the next afternoon to the County Morgue. She didn't like it either and gave a nasty backfire as we pulled into the parking lot.

I opened the door marked "County Medical Examiner's Office" and was met at the reception office by a stern, bifocal middle–aged lady with auburn hair, combed straight back, and sharp, piercing eyes behind large, thick glasses.

Perfect, I thought. If any playwright were casting for a part of the coroner's assistant in "Murder in the County Morgue" she would be it. I expected her to take my pulse as I stood there.

"Perhaps I can help you," she said in monologue fashion.

"I'd like to see Dr. Spiegle, the County Medical Examiner," I said. "I'm Mike Dunn of the *Oakland Herald*. I showed her my ID to convince her.

"Just a minute I'll see if Dr. Spiegle can see you now." she said.

He'd better, I thought. His name was always prominently mentioned in the crime stories of the Herald. His appointment came from the Board of County Commissioners and the Herald was an important link in Board business.

She came back, gave me that same strange look, and said, "He'll see you, go right in."

I looked at a tall, gaunt man with wavy black hair. His manner was precise and methodical. He talked with a slight sneer in his voice as if anything I had to say or do was far below his superior intelligence and education. I can't say that I liked Dr. Spiegel but I had a job to do and had to bear with him.

"Doctor, I'm here about the Tommy Furman case—the 15 year old Whitfield Township boy found dead in a field after a drinking party."

"I'm familiar with the case, what do you want to know?"

"To begin with, I'm a little bit on the minus side as to what your office did with Tommy's body after you picked him up in the field. What did you find?"

The good doctor licked his lips, hunched his shoulders, and prepared to deliver a lesson in anatomy. It was almost as if he was a professor at Michigan State, I was a lowly freshman, and he was about to give his daily lecture.

"The victim was brought here by ambulance after being properly prepared. The body was tagged by the morgue attendant and placed in a refrigerated room until such time as it was removed for further examination."

The doctor was coldly scientific not much color to his "lecture" but I let him go on. My exam grade, anyhow, would come from facts not background color. I didn't want to miss any detail, any little piece of information that might be important in spite of the droll presentation.

Dully the doctor went on, his monotonous sentences spilling out from emotionless face and fish eyes that stared straight ahead with little expression. It was difficult to keep my mind alert.

"Photographs were placed on file that had been taken at the death scene." He emphasized his point by pulling out a file of pictures from a nearby file cabinet. "This photograph of the victim shows him lying partly on his back with the legs twisted somewhat to the left, with his clothes lying in a pile This is a picture from the back looking toward the head and feet. This is a side picture of the face and the puffy lip. This is a close–up of the back with the scratches on it."

"And in your examination and these photographs," I said, "What did you find out about the body of Tommy Furman?"

The doctor evidently wasn't paying attention. Matter–of–factly he continued with his lecture. Taking notes with a thesis

ly he continued with his lecture. Taking notes with a thesis book instead of a regular reporter's notebook, I asked again. He complied this time.

"My examination showed the body was a well developed male that measured 60 inches in height and weighed an estimated 110 pounds. There was lividity present and the lividity was most marked anteriorly."

Again the little smirk of smugness.

"Anteriorly—that means the front of the body."

I answered the remark with a shrug of indifference.

"There was some blanching of the cheek on the right side. There were in addition some superficial scratches of the right anterior wrist and an ecchymosis of the left upper and left lower lip."

"Thanks for the lecture, doctor, now please explain what lividity is."

My little snide remark didn't register well with him. He wanted to play the role of the superior being and I wasn't playing the game right. I had better be careful, I thought, or I would lose the whole interview.

"I'm sorry doctor, please continue."

He picked up the conversation again, but the remark had cut him and he looked at me with contempt.

"Lividity is the discoloration that is produced after death when blood, which is a fluid, seeks its own level. The blood will seep to the lower portion after death. By determining the lividity or where it's located you can determine the position of the body at the time the person died, whether he was on his back or front."

"After conducting your external examination did you conduct an internal examination?"

This would be a key part of the interview—it would indicate how bodily organs were functioning before death, perhaps pinpoint the causes. I hunched forward intently, listening on every word.

"Yes I did. Incisions were made into the body and internal organs examined including the brain."

"In your examination of the organs what was your opinion of the cause of death?"

"It is my opinion that the cause of death was exposure to the elements due to Ethanol Ingestion."

"And how did you arrive at this conclusion?"

"Here we have a young, healthy adolescent with a soft, flabby dilated heart, a swollen brain and pink lungs. These and the lividity that was present on the body which was extremely intense, extremely red which is very typical of a person or persons who die as a result of exposure to the elements."

"How did you arrive at the Ethanol Ingestion conclusion?"

"There was Ethanol present in the body. The amount that was present at the autopsy is significant. It is my opinion that at the time this person arrived in that position he was significantly 'under the influence,' close to intoxication through the use of alcoholic beverages, so that death ensued over a period of time, causing him to be exposed, to remain in the exposed situation."

A question prickled in the back of my mind.

"Correct me if I'm wrong, doctor, but it's my understanding that the normal person, say one who was not 'under the influence,' if he falls asleep and it gets cold, would he wake up?"

I intended the question to determine the degree of intoxication and if because of it Tommy was able to or not able to respond to the ordinary 'survival' beckoning of the human body.

"This is true," he said. "Ordinarily the body would respond to its environment and take measures to avoid its own demise. In an intoxicated person, particularly where the body is in a semi comatose state, it might not, could not and would not take these safety measures."

"Doctor, measuring the blood/alcohol content of the body is a means of determining the intoxication of a person, is it not?"

"Yes. In background, blood, or alcohol is purged from the

body at a relatively fixed rate. And that fixed rate is .015 volumes percent per hour. Given a situation where a person has a certain amount of blood in their blood stream and they cease taking alcoholic beverages the blood will be used primarily by the liver and the alcohol will disappear over a period of time from the blood. We call this purging "Metabolism." It is a term frequently used in Toxicology. To metabolize a substance refers to its degradation by a living organism, changing it from a more complex substance to a simpler substance with the release of energy. In the case of drugs and alcohol and poisons it usually is an attempt to convert a toxic substance into a nontoxic one or to put it into a form easier for the body to eliminate."

"When you speak of Toxicology is that a field concerned with the human body's rate of metabolism of Ethyl Alcohol or Ethanol?"

"Yes it is."

"And in your long experience, plus training in Toxicology, are you familiar with not only the percentage factor concerned with Metabolism but its background?"

"Yes I am."

I was searching for answers but it wasn't easy. I was operating in an unknown field, like probing for treasure without a map. I grabbed for a lead. Anything.

"Suppose, doctor, we were to take a hypothetical situation, and given a certain set of factors could we determine the time that a certain person would have metabolized the alcohol completely so as to bring the blood level back to zero?"

"If the factors are substantiated and the quantities known, yes."

"All right. Let's assume we take a young boy, 15 years of age, weighing around 110–120 pounds, 5 feet in height, and reasonable good heath. Suppose that boy consumed seven 12 ounce beers over a period of 4 1/2 hours, specifically from 6:00 p.m. to 10:30 p.m. on a given night. Could you estimate the highest blood level that individual would have attained and the time in which his blood level would have returned to zero after 10:30 p.m.?"

"You could if you knew several variables."

"What are these variables?"

"The contents of the Gastric GI tract would influence the rate of absorption of alcohol. Having consumed fantastically greasy meals, eating a quarter and a half of butter could delay the rate of absorption of ethyl alcohol, also the percentage of alcohol consumed—was it 3.2 percent, 6 percent beer or what? I would have to know the exact amount of alcohol presented to the system. If the person vomited, this, too would reduce the amount of alcohol presented for metabolizing."

"I don't know all of these factors so we'll have to skip that." I said

Another lead blown where would it end? I threw a final question.

"By the way, what was the blood/alcohol percentage in Tommy's body when he was found?"

".07."

"Is that below the legal level of intoxication?"

"Yes, that is .10. But remember that is the amount in the body when it was found. The rate probably was higher, maybe .23—.26, at the highest level of intoxication. Remember the Metabolism factor.

"Okay. Say the factor was .23—.26, what would be the out-ward symptoms of a person at that blood/alcohol level?"

"There would be slurring of speech, difficulty in locomotion, periods of consciousness and unconsciousness and periods of excitement as well. The mind coordination would also be poor. A factor of .21 in a 15 year old boy would mean that he was ex-tremely drunk, staggering, incoherent, perhaps completely disoriented as to the time, place and environment. He would likely be alternately dozing and coming to. If such a person had a .21

blood/alcohol and went outside in the midst of February temperatures of between 35–40 degrees and laid down on the ground that
had been exposed over a long period of time to low temperatures
unless he was well insulated from air and ground, his body
temperature would fall off rapidly."

"What if he were wearing blue jeans, a T–shirt, long sleeved
shirt and light denim vest, what would happen to that person's
body heat?" I asked.

"Under those conditions, plus the frozen ground that would
extract heat from the body I would say the loss of body heat would
be rapid," he said. "Once the body heat gets low enough, and that's
around 90–92 degrees, the person would go into hypothermia,
unable to help himself and death would ensue. And that's what
caused his death. Hypothermia caused by incapacity due to acute
alcoholism."

The doctor was growing restless. He had about reached the
end of his patience. The lecture hour was about to end. To go on
further I would probably only be getting short, unmeaningful
answers that would go nowhere. It was time to leave.

"Thank you doctor, I must be going," I said.

"I'd like to see your story before you print it," he said.

A good newspaperman never gets into that trap. By the time
the interviewee looks over your work, you could be rewriting the
whole story. Besides that you risk the chance that he might want
to delete something important. What would a coroner know about
writing a news story any more than I would about dissecting a
body? It was time for my own lecture.

"Doctor," I said. "I know you're concerned about the truth
and so am I. Professionally I've been a newspaper writer in this
area for 10 years. You've been Medical Examiner for this county
for eight years. That makes my score a plus two. Don't you think
by now if anything had been wrong with my writing that here it
would have shown? I don't know of any writer who shows his
stories in advance. It's professional ethics involved like a doc-

tor/patient relationship or lawyer/client. Besides, if you detect anything wrong with my story, you have a perfect right to ask for a correction—and the Herald has always been fair on this."

"You may be right. I only wanted to make sure that it's the truth."

"Fine, so do I. We'll leave it at that."

# Chapter 8

"Medical Examiner Theorizes on Tommy's last Moments," the headline read in The Herald the next day. I tried in writing to be conservative. It was a story about a young man, dazed and incoherent, wandering aimlessly in a field. It left Tommy's final acts up for conjecture but carried several possible theories. It wasn't a pretty story and it carried an underlying theme of "nobody cared." It was clear, the story said, that when Tommy passed out in the bathroom the invisible line between mischief and danger had long since been crossed. The story added, "this is not one of those stories someone will tell with nostalgia when they are recounting all their boyish pranks after they have grown up to be older and wiser."

I had hardly settled down to read it after the press run had started when my desk phone rang.

It was that mysterious voice again, the one that said my article was wrong about Hunter mingling with the guests at the party.

The voice was unrecognizable. Maybe the caller was using a handkerchief over his mouth. It could have been Humphrey Bogart, Carol Channing, or Bob Hope, for all I knew.

"Do you want a big scoop on the Furman case?" the voice said.

"If you have any additional information, other than what has been written, yes." I said.

"Then ask Mike Dooley about what happened to Tommy in his pick up truck."

The voice trailed off and I had a feeling my caller was about to end the conversation quickly unless I acted.

"Wait a minute, what about —"

Click then silence.

Mike Dooley, I thought, wasn't he one of the teenagers at the party? The name rang a bell but was still out of focus. A quick

check with Sgt. Hansard provided the answer. He was a sopho-
more student at Whitfield High and yes; he had been at the party.
It was a new lead and worth checking. I called the school office,
inquired where I could get in touch with him. It was then after
school but the school office remained open until 4:00 p.m. They
said he had just left for football practice. I had a routine assignment in the area. I could stop off at the practice field afterwards.

When I arrived at the field Whitfield's young coach had just
delivered one of those Monday afternoon 'Vince Lombardi' type
of lectures to the team after its disastrous loss to rival Fenton High
School on Friday night. An English teacher would have been
shocked at the choice of words. But to a football player, it was
merely a "chewing out" talk, something to take in stride like
getting conked on the helmet when the coach took you out for a
bad play.

It was nearly the end of practice so I waited patiently while
the coach roughed out his game plan for the next contest. I idly
watched while the players lined up and ran a play. The quarterback
yelled "hup hup" and suddenly there were grunts and groans.
Bodies crunched and shoulder pads popped. A player didn't get
up. Other players gathered around him as he clutched his back and
stomach, groaning in pain. He was back on his feet in 10 minutes
ready for action. The coach nodded approvingly and gave him a
clop on the helmet.

Practice ended the players, helmets in hand, started to walk
off the field. I asked one of them where Mike Dooley was and he
pointed to a red haired, freckled face young man with huge
shoulders and neck that didn't seem to start anywhere or end
anywhere.

"Hey Mike," I shouted. The head turned and a pair of brown,
intense eyes stared questioningly at me.

"I'd like to talk to you a minute." I said.

He loped over to me, nervously scratched his head, wiped
the sweat off his brow, and said: "About what?"

"About Tommy Furman and the party at Twin Oaks Ranch."

The face scowled immediately. His answers started to come defensively.

"I don't think I can tell you much. I didn't see him too much at the party and besides that stuff that has been rumored about me is a vicious lie. Who are you?"

"I'm sorry, Mike Dunn of the *Oakland Herald*."

A puzzled frown came to the face. I had another 'lecture' in mind to erase it.

"Look you don't have to talk to me. But if what you say is true about the rumor, wouldn't you like to get it out to people and let them know it is a lie?"

It was a trick reporters sometimes use to get people to open up. And it made a lot of sense. You can't fight rumors with silence. It's like trying a case in court. First you have a witness facing direct examination and then comes the cross–examination for rebuttal. In actual life the newspaper acts as the place and opportunity where rebuttals take place. People talk a lot about cases 'being tried in the newspaper.' But try and put a gag on everyone and see what happens. In many instances unknown witnesses, important to the case, come forward with evidence after reading about it in the newspapers.

"I never thought of it that way, I guess, but yes, maybe I should give my side," he said.

I motioned to a player's bench and I started with the questions.

"What about this so–called rumor about you and Tommy and the back of the pick up truck?"

I was fishing for a lead. Those were the only two things I had heard about his situation. But he grabbed the line and ran.

He looked away. It was a full minute before the words came.

"Okay," he said. "This is how it happened. I heard that Tommy was real bad so my girl friend and I went out to the truck to check on him. He was shaking real bad, like he was nervous or something, like maybe he had a cold or something. He kept shaking. I heard he had been 'dry heavin' in the bathroom. He didn't seem to be sick to his stomach in the truck, though, just kept shaking. I asked him if he was all right and stuff but he didn't answer, just kept shaking and stuff. Earlier I had seen him laying in the mud and with mud all over his T shirt."

"Did you touch him when you checked him over?"

"Yeah. We tried to shake him and he tried to talk but something was wrong with him. My girlfriend and me thought we might sober him up by going for a ride in the cold air. We covered him up with a blanket and cruised around the area for awhile and when we got back we checked on him and the tail gate was down and Tommy was gone."

"What happened then?"

"We got back in the truck and retraced our route. We found him passed out. Put him back in the truck and brought him back to the 'Ranch.' Later we heard that he had gotten out of the truck and somehow gotten back to the party again. They rumored that we left Tommy out there in a field in the cold but that's not true."

What's the difference whether you left him in a field or in the back of a truck, I thought.

Then I added: "Was there some kind of fight going on between Tommy and you?"

"That was another rumor that wasn't true. Actually it was Tommy and Rod Ainsworth who were involved. I heard Rod was getting rowdy because Tommy was getting drunk and butting in on his conversation with a girl. I heard he pushed Tommy up against the wall and stuff."

"Did you know ahead of time that there would be beer and alcoholic beverages at the party?"

"Yeah, we all knew it."

"Was Mr. Hunter in the bathroom when Tommy was 'dry heaving?'"

"I don't remember. I know he made some kind of statement

like 'someone should take care of that kid before something happens.'"

"When you last saw Tommy, was his lip bruised or puffed?"

"No, not that I seen."

"Was there Marijuana smoking going on at the party outside the 'Ranch'?"

"Well, there was seven or eight of us outside hitting on a joint. But don't print that, it could get me kicked off the team. We only got one hit on it, though, before it was gone."

"Did you see much of Tommy at the party?"

"I saw him when he first came in. He and Bill Jeremy had a bottle of Southern Comfort. Bill said they had been passing it back and forth, drinking on the way to the party. I heard it was about half gone when they arrived. Then a couple of us took a 'hit' on it. Tommy and I got mad at Rod because he drank a whole bunch and we didn't want him to kill the bottle."

"What do you mean by a 'hit?'"

"I mean a 'hit,' a 'slug.'"

He demonstrated by putting his thumb up to his mouth and leaving it there for an instant.

"Would you describe the party as orderly or out of control?"

"It was a typical teen party. We were all standin' around and drinking and talking. Having fun, you know. There wasn't a lot of wild partying around. We were just minding our own business."

"Was there anything going on outside except the Marijuana business?"

"Well, someone was out there with about five or six kids and trying to teach them Karate kicks. They were just laughing and having a good time. We were just having fun, Mr. Dunn, minding our own business, not hurting anybody. Just kids having a good time," he said.

Verbally, I had just been to a teenage drinking party. It was shocking in some ways, not so shocking in other ways. How much did it differ from the Christmas office party, the neighborhood beach party on Labor Day? Somehow the thought kept banging back in my mind from the last story about when the invisible line between mischief and danger ceases.

# Chapter 9

"You've been doing a lot of work on the Furman case concerning teenage parties, how'd you like to do a feature on it?"

It was my regional editor talking. He must have been reading my mind. The thought had been bugging me ever since the interview with Mike Dooley. It had all kinds of possibilities; the responsibility of parents at parties, how to control teenagers without having them get belligerent at you; what to look for in drug reactions, and much more.

"Sounds fine," I said. "When do I start?"

"Right now. You set it up. You've already got background to start with. Take it from there."

I thought I knew the right man to see. He was Police Chief Bill Berryman of the Whitfield Police Department. He not only knew background from the Whitfield area but before coming to Whitfield, he had had extensive work with juveniles from the Oakland County Juvenile Court system. Besides he was a personal friend I knew when I worked on the weekly Whitfield Gazette.

A phone call renewed our acquaintanceship, and when I mentioned the subject, he was more than glad to oblige.

Once again I found myself in the village of Whitfield, this time headed for the local police station.

The dispatcher greeted me at the entranceway and said the chief was waiting.

I shook his hand and we both settled down to comfortable positions. He was a young, rather tall man with black hair and black moustache, closely clipped and neat. He talked rapidly but paused often, gathering his thoughts and letting them sink in before going on—or was he just being extra careful and diplomatic in talking with the press?

"Just how extensive are teenage parties in this area, or any other area, and what are the pitfalls of parents who host them?" I began.

"You mean 'grassers' or home parties?" he asked.

"I guess I mean all of them. What are 'grassers?'"

"They're usually held in a large field. One or two kids decide to throw one and the word circulates quickly by mouth. They'll gather at the appointed hour and everyone brings a six pack of beer or bottle of wine, a fifth, and a stereo. Between the booze, the wine or beer and the loud music I guess they get their kicks. We know these parties are going on most of the time and there is a place at Rattalee Lake Road and Bone Roads that seems to be a headquarters area. But we're powerless to do anything about it. It's out of our jurisdiction. Although they start with four or five kids, I've seen as many as 200 in a field. They're not supervised and most of them are minors. The biggest problem we have is policing them and finding out when they're going to happen. That, and trying to break them up. We can't go on private property, you know, unless they're breaking an ordinance like being too loud or creating a disturbance. If it's a house party and we get a call that someone is creating a disturbance, we have to knock on the door, identify ourselves as police officers, and ask them to quiet down. But we can't go in to check around unless the person opening the door creates a disturbance or gives us a hard time."

"What kind of suggestions do you have for parents who host teenage parties?" I asked.

"First of all, know your children's friends. Make sure they are morally respectable in the community. Give them a lecture before the party—no booze or alcoholic beverages will be allowed. Circulate upstairs, downstairs or wherever they are to make sure everything is in control. Be firm, don't let anyone tell you you're an old Fogie for not letting things get out of control.

"What about drugs?"

"That's a definite problem. Some kids are pretty naive. They'll put an upper or downer in a drink just to see the reaction. Some kids have been known to offer a friend a cigarette from a package. The cigarette turns out to be a joint. Personally I don't know how that can happen. I can detect a joint a couple of rooms away. Some say they smell sweet, others claim they smell like burnt rope, others burnt almonds."

"They say that teenage drinking is filtering down to the junior high level, is that true?"

"You're damned right it is. The other day we were searching the Junior High lockers—we had a legal right to do so in this case—and we found a half empty fifth of Scotch, with a girl lookin' on. Most of the parents try to act responsible. They lecture the kids ahead of time, tell them that drinking will be strictly limited and mingle with the kids. I know of one parent who got wind somehow that her teenage daughter was at a drinking party and she went right over, grabbed her daughter, and took her home. But then, there are the unchaperoned parties."

"What do you mean?"

"I mean when the parents go away for the weekend and their kids decide to throw a party. The word gets around and then you got a wild one on your hands."

"How do you combat that?"

"You talk to the neighbors and tell them to check on the situation, that you're leaving for a few days and would they watch over things. You talk to your children, tell them that you won't stand for any partying, and hope that you've earned their respect enough that they'll obey your wishes. Then you leave and pray."

"Just how extensive are these parties?"

"We're not that naive to not know that they're going on. The problem time is always at graduation. Dad remembers back to the time when he graduated. He just assumes that he would be old fashioned if he didn't allow the kids to do what he did in the 'good old days.' It seems; too, that kids have grown used to the idea of booze around the house. Dad's watching the football game on TV with a can of beer in his hands. Junior comes up and dad gives him a drink out of the can. It happens in early childhood. Dad opens the refrigerator and pulls out a can of beer. Soon junior knows that he can do the same thing. It's ingrained in our system, I guess. But the big thing is not to overdo it."

"Do you have an on–going program to prevent teenage alcoholism and drugs?" I asked.

"We certainly do. But we've changed our thoughts on that, too. One time we had a lecture/demonstration on drugs. Brought all of the paraphernalia, the pipes, the syringes, the rolling papers and everything else. Showing them how to do it only added to the problem even though we tried to show the dangers. We had more drug related cases after the demonstration than before. One thing that did help, however, was a program put on by a group out of Milford, called the 'Palmer Drug Abuse Program.' Some of the youths that had become addicts came over and talked to our kids, telling about how their life had been nearly ruined and their health endangered. It had quite an effect on our kids. It was definitely a good move on our part."

The chief shifted his position as he warmed to the subject. Now both of his long legs were sprawled on the desk and he leaned back in his chair in a philosophical mood.

"But the problem isn't drugs, it's alcohol. The majority of kid's act just like their old man. It's a bad deal to get high on drugs, but to get boozed up, that's just part of growing up. Dad brags about getting 'crocked' at the high school homecoming game when he was young and he tells about the wild times at the (office Christmas) party. How in hell can he lecture to his kid about booze when he was guilty of the same thing when he was a teenager? And when junior says he can drink five bottles of beer without even feeling it dad is likely to say 'when I was your age I could drink seven.' And dad talks about when he was young and staying out all night, taking a quick shower in the morning and heading for a regular day's work on the old assembly line, like it was a big thing to be able to hold your 'likker' and not show it. Michigan law provides that alcoholic liquor shall not be sold or furnished to a person unless the person has attained 21 years of age. A person who knowingly sells or furnishes alcoholic liquor to a minor under 21 or fails to make a diligent inquiry as to whether the person is less than 21 is guilty of a misdemeanor. The Michigan Court of Appeals recently ruled that this status applies to private individuals as well as commercial establishments. But conviction as a misdemeanor means only 90 days, even if the party ends up with death or serious injury. We had a case right here in Whitfield where a young man went to a graduation party where adults furnished the liquor. He didn't drink very much, but he made a fatal mistake, one that cost him his life—he went home with someone who had been drinking heavily. Their car hit a tree. The driver came out of it all right, but the kid, who was his passenger, died."

Chief Berryman's theories on teenage alcohol and drug abuse were very interesting but time was getting short. I stole a glance at my watch; it was nearly 5:00 p.m. and time to get back to the apartment. I had what I wanted, an interesting story with a vital moral message. The chief slid his long legs off the table and I ended the interview with a handshake and thanks.

# Chapter 10

I had hardly settled down to a story about "TEENAGE DRINK-ING PARTIES ON THE INCREASE" when my desk phone rang again.

"Hello," I said absently, my mind still on my story.

"Are you Mike Dunn?"

I hunched forward alertly. It was the same voice that had hung up on me after telling me about Tommy being in the bed of the pick up truck.

"Yes—and you are the same guy that hung up on me the last time," I said.

"I know," the voice said. "I was too scared the last time, I mean, I didn't want to get involved."

"So what's so different this time?"

"My wife. I had a long talk with my wife about the case and she said I should tell you what I know about it."

"And what do you know about it?"

"I don't want to tell you over the phone. Meet me some-where," the voice said.

"Where?"

"Let's see, I'm going to be later this afternoon near the Edgewood Plaza Shopping Center. I can meet you there—at the entrance to the Kohler Men's Store, about 4:00 p.m."

I looked at my schedule; everything had been wrapped up. It was after deadline time and I was free to go so I answered: "Okay, see you there. By the way, what's your name and how will I know you?"

"My name's Garcia and I own a bar. Victor Garcia. I'll be wearing a T–shirt that says "Garcia's Bar. It's my bowling shirt."

"Can you give me some inkling of what's this all about? I don't want to go on a wild goose chase."

"I can't tell you everything but it's about some guys who

73

were talking about the case in my bar two nights ago."

"Sounds important, I'll see you there."

The mall was only a few blocks from the paper so after I had wound things up on my 'Teenage Drinking Parties' story, cleaned up a couple of minor features and a brief government story, I wheeled the Mustang over and wheezed Mert into a parking lot close to the entranceway.

The Mall was pretty much like any other Mall, an arched entranceway branching out like a fan with stores on each side. I entered and looked at trades people and carpenters entering and leaving, with tools, materials, and pieces of equipment in hand. The Mall was being renovated to keep up with new designs.

Ah progress, I thought.

Everything was now being constructed under a 10–year plan. Ten years and it's out like a shoe that needs resoling.

What ever happened to durability? My dad's old linotype was 50 years old and still running good, turning out job printing type. You can't even buy parts for modern day typesetting machines after 10 years. They're obsolete.

I remember when I was growing up in Whitfield and used to marvel at the uniqueness of its Main street. You walked down town and each building had a distinct design, a different size and personality of its own. The barbershop had a revolving candy striped pole in a glass globe, the hardware store a sign with a hammer and saw. On some of the old buildings artistic cornices graced their upper regions. When you went through Whitfield you spent a moment or two just gazing at its artistic buildings.

In contrast, a neighboring town completed a modernization movement a few years ago. The town fathers decided to make it like a shopping mall. Down came the magnificent buildings. Squat, lifeless rectangular one story shaped buildings replaced them and immediately people said they felt a coldness to the town, like a body without a face. In fact a couple of people who had set out to visit relatives said they completely missed the town because they thought it was a factory.

Inside the Mall, shoppers were rushing everywhere with artistic printed shopping bags. Every place had a sale going on except Wendy's Hamburger restaurant. How gullible can people get, I thought. It was an old merchandising trick, displaying merchandise in the window at a ridiculously high price for a week, then lowering it "by sale" to its regular price while the suckers poured in. A hometown merchant once told me that an incensed lady came into his shop and said what did he mean by selling this coat so high. She said she had seen the same coat in a nearby Mall advertised in the paper for one third less. The merchant couldn't believe it; he was just taking a fair markup; the other firm must have been selling it below cost. Deciding to investigate he went into the store, spotted the coat on a hanger. It looked exactly like his but checking closer he found that it had no lining.

I had little time before my meeting with Garcia so I decided to sit for awhile on the edge of a glittering water fountain constructed with a cement slab along the outer edge where people could sit and 'People Watch.'

I looked up and a tall, gangling kid with a loud stereo walked gimpy legged down a promenade in front of the stores. The stares of the disturbed people around him had no effect as he haphazardly swung the stereo backward and forward to match his gait. The music faded with him like the fadeout of a popular record on the radio before the last note sounded.

I looked over to a children's shoe shop. Like some Mall stores It had no front window so it was easy to see what was going on inside.

A little Chinese man sat behind a huge cash register, his body barely visible. A pencil was on his ear and he had been doing some bookkeeping to keep busy.

A shopper and her young daughter entered the shop and he walked to meet them. There was some kind of discussion about shoe style, the young girl wasn't satisfied, and the twosome left.

The little man went back to his bookkeeping, this time with a worried frown on his face. An ordinary little scene with ordinary people. A minor episode along the road of life.

A fat lady overloaded with packages puffed to a seat beside me. Her face was red and perspiring. She paused to catch her breath, took out a compact and proceeded to make up her face while dozens of people paraded by, uninterested. A little old man with a disheveled suit, in which the pants and jacket didn't match, looked absently around and sat down. He, too, was people watching. I don't think he had much else to do that day, anyhow.

As I sat there psychoanalyzing everyone, like a psychiatrist with endless clients sitting on a couch, my keen eyes observed that there are three classes of people who frequent shopping malls: those who have something definite in mind to buy; those who come for lack of nothing else to do and those who want to be entertained while they shop. The endless model airplane shows, the antique shows, the art shows, and such, attract the latter.

I get restless "People Watching" and decided to take a stroll. I had about 10 minutes before my meeting.

I walked past the Kohler's Men's Fashion Department. On my way I passed a department store facial makeup counter. The woman in charge was applying rouge and eyeshade to a willing customer who had a face that was a cross between a Boston Bull Dog and a Golden Retriever. Nothing, I observed, could improve that face. But the clerk was doing her best, observing, "I think you need a lighter eye shade to contrast with your darker eyes and slightly more rouge on the cheeks to give you more color."

The scene interested me so much that I must have been guilty of staring. Both suddenly looked up at me and my face flushed. I hurried away as fast as I could walk.

After a quick glance at Men's fashions I quickly looked at my watch and saw it was time to head back.

I positioned myself at the entranceway, arms akimbo, and suddenly he appeared in view.

"Garcia's Bar" was in large blue letters on a yellow shirt—I couldn't miss it.

He was rather short, thin black hair and heavy jowl face. Like all people peculiar to his trade he had a bulging stomach, probably from consuming too many beers with bar friends. In my mind I could see him, leg hunched on a bar stool, white apron and sleeves rolled halfway up to his elbows, talking to a patron about the latest Lions football game. I almost expected him to say, "What's yours?" instead of the, "Is your name Mike Dunn?" opener that he threw at me.

"That's me" I said and motioned him to follow me to a nearby Wendy's, about the only place in the mall where you could sit down at a table.

We sat down and ordered coffee from a lifeless, short dumpy waitress; then we dallied with the spoons as we sought a mutual meeting ground on conversation.

"I'm sorry I can't offer you a Stroh's but you chose the meeting place." I offered lightly, hoping to set the mood.

"That's all right," he said, "I like to get away from the smoke and atmosphere of a bar once in a while."

"Tell me about your friends and their conversation about Tommy Furman at your bar." I said. It was time to get down to the crux of the meeting.

"Well there was three guys at the bar, all young looking, but old enough to drink. I know because I checked their ID's. He emphasized this, perhaps thinking I might be an investigative newsman looking for a scoop about bars that sell drinks to underage teenagers.

"I couldn't help but hear them," he said, "because I was close to them as I am to you right now. An you know, I'm cleaning up the spilled drinks, wiping the bar, and that sort of stuff so it's not like I'm eavesdropping."

"Go on."

"Well this one guy is saying something about the big party

at Twin Oaks and how he was at it and about the Furman boy being found out in the field dead, and stuff. Then he mentions something about Tommy being in a terrific fight that night, about being pushed up against a door and getting a few fists in the face by someone called Rod Hinsley. The guy said Tommy was beat up pretty bad, got a fat lip out of it and a smashed face. He said Tommy left after the beating and he didn't see him afterwards."

"And?"

"Well I read about the case in your newspaper and I thought that since you carried a byline on the story you might like to know about it. My wife and I were talking about it and she thought I should get in touch with you."

"How come you came to me? Why didn't you go to the Prosecuting Attorney or the Sheriff's Department?"

"Well you know, I didn't want to get involved. I thought you could write one of those stories without using anybody's name, you know, like—"

"According to a usually reliable source who wishes to remain anonymous?" I said.

"Yea, that's it."

It hit me suddenly the Herald had recently run an editorial about this type of reporting. The editorial criticized some members of the media who were hiding behind such terms and that people who read newspapers are entitled to know that authority is being quoted so they can see for themselves whether the authority quoted is actually reliable or not.

"What makes you think that I want to use that approach?" I asked. "My editor is getting touchy about this type of reporting."

"Well I'm not going to the Prosecuting Attorney and I'm not going to the Sheriff's Department. I guess, then, I just won't talk. I told you I don't want to get involved. You can take it or shove it."

"What makes you think that this might have anything to do with the case, anyhow." I said, stalling for time.

"Well, me and my wife think this fight definitely has something to do with Tommy's death. Like he might have died not only from the booze but the effects of the fight. I've seen it in my bar dozens of times. A guy gets juiced up, gets in a fight, gets beat up and unless someone takes him home he's in no shape to go anywhere. That could have happened to that young boy. Both the booze and getting beat up could have caused his death."

"So you want me to keep you out of it, but use your information." I said.

"If you want to, yes."

The argument lingered in my mind. Could I get away with it? The story was too good to leave out. I would have to check it with the kid in the fight, but it was an interesting theory.

"Okay, you win. But if my editor decides otherwise you may be hearing from me again." I said.

Both of us were running out of time. We exchanged some chitchat information, finished our coffee, shook hands and left.

As I left I noticed the little old man was still sitting near the water fountain. He didn't even look like he had moved from the same position. The dinner hour would soon be approaching and he would have to leave. But to where? A relative's place perhaps? A lonely apartment or room? It must be terrible, I thought, to arrive at a station in life where all you had to look forward to was "People Watching" at a Mall, go to an afternoon movie or sit on a park bench feeding pigeons.

In a story involving controversy a reporter had better be sure of his facts. An absolute essential is contacting the other party to get the other side.

It was time to pay a call on Rod Hinsley.

Hinsley, I found out later, was one of those so-called teenage dropouts. The kind that leave school early in life, can't pick up a career and seem to drift between jobs because of inexperience. They also seem to return to the scene of earlier "Buddy relationships," school orientated extra curricular activities, hovering on the perimeter of school dances when they can sneak in and the football games where they gather with other dropouts on the edge of the playing field. They never seem to have anything to do except wander around town, play games at the electronic arcades, the pool hall or billiards parlor.

A call to his home revealed that Rod wasn't there but was downtown at the local arcade. His mother didn't know when he would be home but she was sure he would still be there. Rod didn't vary his routine much in the afternoon unless he was working. He played games until about 5:30 p.m., returned home for supper and then disappeared to God knows where. His mother's voice was short and curt when I asked her where he was. I guessed she didn't have much control over him. Like the shifting wind Rod was a victim of his whims, wherever they would take him.

Whitfield isn't too far from the Edgewood Plaza, about a 15–minute drive. I decided to chance it that I would find him there, besides the "Twofers" hour was on at that time at the Whitfield Hotel. It wasn't that much of a decision.

The familiar Whitfield Party store loomed on the windshield of the Mustang, and I parked on the Main Street. The Whitfield Arcade had received the blessing of the city fathers to operate downtown under a franchise limiting its occupants to non school–age youngsters during the daytime, while the school students could come in after school, up to 10:00 p.m.

Entering the darkened arcade from bright sunlight didn't do my eyes any good. It took a good half–minute before they adjusted. When they focused I saw a dozen or more youths in various stages of posture ranging from sloppy to upright alertness. The room was filled with electronic sounds, bomb bursts, bells that rang out, popular tunes of the day when an exceptional play was made, and the banshee sound of a jet engine under full acceleration. The players seemed in a trance, eyes glued to the video screen, bodies pulsating in jerky motions and heads turning in all directions like a robot whose condensers started malfunctioning.

On the screen strange little figures ate each other up as they traveled up and down, sideways and through all kinds of traps designed to send an unwary space traveler into the depths of the fifth dimension.

It was a teenager's paradise. For the price of four bits one could shoot down speeding asteroids, send invading space ships into infinity with a blast of a space gun or even drive a speeding car through all kinds of police barricades, maybe gleefully smashing a couple of patrol cars in the process. Imagine the happiness a teenager experiences in running down his favorite "Fuzz." All for four bits.

I walked up to the cashier's window and asked if he knew where Rod Hinsley was. He motioned me to a machine called "Space Traveler" where a rather heavy set, medium height young man with an unkempt red beard was in the middle of a space journey to Saturn. I drew up along side of him and said: "Are you Rod Hinsley?"

"Yeah, whatta you want?"

"I'd like to ask you about Tommy Furman and the Twin Oaks party."

I saw his back immediately stiffen and his eyes averted me as the statement sank in. He went back to his game, saying nothing.

"Would you like to know what people are saying about you and Tommy? I asked.

"Whatever they're saying it's a damn lie. Fuck them, they're all liars."

"Look, I'm Mike Dunn of the *Oakland Herald*. If you really want to get back at your so–called friends who are badmouthing you, talk to me. I'll print most of everything you say that is the truth, but you had better not lie to me. He looked at my eyes thinking but not seeing.

"Okay, if you print what I say, I'll talk to you."

"I didn't say I would print everything you say," I said. "I would print the truth as you say it. Now let's get out of here where we can talk. This place is giving me the creeps."

He aimed the space gun for one final shot, 'zapped' an invading Martian ship, slapped the machine lovingly with his hand and said: "Let's go."

I led him to a nearby drug store, "Mac's Pharmacy" where they had tables and a place to sit down and talk. It was the town's headquarters for conversation. In fact I used to get some of my lead stories here. My friend, Barb, who waited on tables, had a pipeline to everything that was newsworthy in Whitfield.

We sat down and ordered coffee.

"Now tell me about this fight I keep hearing you and Tommy got into at Twin Oaks." I said.

"It wasn't that big a deal," he said. "I got mad at Tommy because he kept butting into a conversation I was having with a few girls. We never asked him over there in the first place, but he kept butting in."

"So what happened?"

"Well, I could see that the girls were getting mad about it so I told him to 'butt out,' but he didn't. He kept right on hogging the conversation, making silly remarks and he was half drunk too. I finally grabbed him by the vest and shook him. He started to give me a sucker punch and I nailed him, right on the lip. I pushed him a couple of more times and he finally broke away and went somewhere else. And that's all there was. I swear it. I don't care what they say."

"Rod, how much did you have to drink at the party?"

"I had two beers, maybe a shot of vodka and five shots of Peppermint Schnapps."

"Could you have been so 'smashed' that you didn't know whether you struck Tommy with a blow that made him senseless, unable to know what he was doing, disorganized?"

"No way. After I hit him he knew I could beat him up so he

just walked away."

"They said he walked away and was never seen again—is that true?"

"No, someone said they saw him in the barnyard after that."

"Did anyone make an attempt to take Tommy home after he became intoxicated?"

"I heard a lot of people say 'we should give him a ride home' but nothing was done about it."

"What was the condition of Mr. Hunter, the host, at the party?"

"Whatta you mean, condition?"

"I mean had he been drinking, was he cold sober, or what?"

"He was cold sober. He was in his bedroom, watchin' television."

"Was he mingling with the guests at the party or was he keeping to his own business?"

"He was keeping to his own business."

"How many of these drinking parties have you observed in your experience?"

"Every other weekend there would be one or two on the average."

# Chapter 11

My headline the next day read: "Teen denies fight had anything to do with Tommy's death."

The case, meanwhile, had reached an impasse. The examination would be next week. From what I had heard, in talking to the Prosecutor, the defense would let their client waive examination and proceed to Circuit Court. They believed they would stand a better chance with a jury trial. Again the old "in the same boat" routine, they thought, where the jury would sympathize with the defendant knowing that they had gone through a similar experience. Mores were difficult to deal with, the conformist pattern at work.

The Prosecutor was right.

Judge Gerald McNulty in 52nd District Court heard their pleadings to waive examination and bound them over to Circuit Court.

The docket being crowded, the case was set for late September.

I covered the examination. Both defendants were silent and drawn. Both said classic "no comments" when the press questioned them. The Furman case was now on hold until fall. And I was glad because I was getting too involved and there were too many unanswered questions and personal issues involved. My mind was cluttered with conflict, like a computer with a shorted wire, where the questions were programmed right, but the answers came out wrong.

It was good to get back into the mainstream of regular reporting; City Commission stories, features, crime and a few 'weirdo's.'

The weirdo was a routine story about a single–car–injury accident. The driver had been slightly intoxicated, ran off the road and into a ditch. Both occupants were injured, their names were duly recorded and I forgot about it—for one day.

The next day I got a telephone call from the lady passenger. She asked for a retraction. Said she wasn't in the car and we had made a terrible mistake. I told her I would check it out, and, if incorrect, the Herald would run a correction.

A check with the local police chief unraveled the mystery. She had been a passenger in the car all right and the story was correct. Turned out she was cheating on her husband, according to the chief. No wonder she wanted the correction.

# Chapter 12

It was getting to be mid summer in Michigan and the news "doldrums" were setting in. Vacations were eating into our staff, and I found myself sent out to cover events not in my regular line of work, nor my area.

As a regional reporter for The Herald I covered a number of township and villages in North Oakland County, Whitfield being one. Normally another reporter was assigned to cover neighboring Groveland Township, but being on vacation, it became my assignment. The monthly township board meeting was my assignment as I set forth in the Mustang.

I arrived at the Groveland Township Hall about 10 minutes before meeting time. It was packed with people. The matter up for discussion was a company seeking to establish a waste disposal plant in the township, a move sure to bring on the wrath of environmentalists who were beginning to pick up strength, not only locally, but nationwide. Not only that, they were attracting a lot of people to their side, including politicians. The issue had definite political overtones, with many votes in balance.

The presentation of the company was smooth and flawless.

The AntiPol Corporation sought a construction permit to start a plant that would convert toxic and hazardous inorganic wastes to an inert material called "Sealosafe," a rock–like substance that would be buried in the ground after processing.

The chemistry involved, they said, is complex but similar to the reaction that takes place in the formation of concrete. They assured the audience that the end product would meet all federal and state standards for non–hazardous materials.

They described a typical plant layout: Regional facilities would receive a wide variety of solid, liquid and sludge wastes, some of which are chemically incompatible. Waste reception and storage areas, therefore, would be segregated according to the type of wastes. Separate areas would be provided for acids, neutral and alkaline wastes, for cyanide and chrome wastes. Bulk solids would be unloaded in an enclosed storage area. Liquids and slurries would be pumped from tank trucks to appropriate reception tanks. Drummed wastes would be separated on arrival and taken up for treatment as required. In theory, it sounded like the answer to long–standing toxic waste problems brought on by modern technological improvements in industry.

From storage facilities the wastes would be conveyed to one of several disintegration centers, depending upon the type of wastes. Drummed wastes, for example, would be conveyed to a drum shredder where the drum and the waste are disintegrated and dispersed in an appropriate liquid. The disintegration stage, a spokesman pointed out, is to prepare a stable dispersion of solid and liquid materials, which is suitable for pretreatment and subsequent conversion to AntiPol material. In the pretreatment process some toxic waste materials would receive chemical pretreatment to prepare them for the final fixation into the Sealosafe process. Then the wastes are prepared for their final process, conversion into a AntiPol material in slurry form, which can then be discharged into an adjacent land reclamation site. The slurry begins to harden within a few hours. After about three days, the product is solid.

During the presentation the audience remained patiently silent. It was a highly technical subject; some of the terms were not familiar and the process was certainly new. Sensing the growing concern and knowing the controversial nature of the issue, Township Board Supervisor Donald Titsworth called for calm and deliberation before turning the meeting over to questions. He warned those in attendance to keep their tempers in line and no one would be allowed to speak over three minutes. There would only be one opportunity to talk in order to give everyone a chance.

The lecture over, he was confronted by a sea of hands.

A farmer in the front row, dressed in bib overalls, voice

trembling because he wasn't used to speaking before a group, asked: "What do we know about this process? I never heard of it before. How do we know if it will work?" His voice calmed and became demanding as he gained confidence in speaking; he wasn't about to be put down.

The company spokesman was ready. He read from a prepared text.

"The Sealosafe technology developed during the early 1970's in England as a result of increasing concern over incorrect disposition of wastes and resulting environmental disasters. England, with its high level of industrialization and population density was among the first countries to recognize the need for improved waste treatment technology. In 1975 the first commercial facility designed specifically to treat inorganic wastes utilizing Sealosafe technology was completed and brought into operation. Since that time other facilities have been brought on stream."

A man in a blue business suit, an opposite of the rough dressed farmer, interrupted: "We can't care about England—what about in the good old USA and especially right here in Groveland Township?"

"I was coming to that," the speaker said, "when the resource and Recovery Act of 1976 was enacted the need for improved waste treatment and disposal technologies was formed to introduce the Sealosafe process here where it will be offered at large regional waste management facilities, on–site facilities dedicated to large waste generators and portable treatment facilities for waste pile and lagoon cleanup."

The questions were coming faster like a car with a stuck accelerator.

"What kind of safeguards do you guys have in case of an accident?"

"You mean an 'Environmental accident'?" the speaker asked.

"I don't care what you call it. I mean if some of the stuff

you're mixing with the water explodes?"

The speaker's face flushed. The question had upset his composure. The answer had escaped his copywriter; wasn't to be found in the neat list of questions and answers they had so carefully prepared. It was a momentary reaction that quickly passed, however. Now he was back in his pre–planned orbit, fighting to keep it.

"First of all, we don't mix wastes indiscriminately." he said. "Each type of waste requires a different processing technique. A representative sample is brought to the laboratory for analysis and formulation development. A thorough chemical analysis is performed, including the determination of heavy metals, cyanide and other determination. With analysis complete a treatment formulation is developed." he said.

"With all of those trucks coming in how do you keep track of each shipment to make sure they don't get mixed?" asked a woman in the back.

"All waste deliveries to the regional AntiPol plant are scheduled and the plant and laboratory personnel are notified in advance. No unscheduled deliveries are accepted," he said.

As more hands shot up the speaker asked for quiet, saying: "Perhaps I can answer many of your questions in one grouping. Let me explain it this way. When a truck enters the plant it moves to the weigh scale; a sample of the waste is taken to the laboratory. While the waste is being analyzed the manifest is checked and the vehicle is weighed. If the analysis and manifest are in order the vehicle is assigned to an unloading station. For bulk liquid deliveries the truck is directed to an unloading area where off–loading is supervised by a plant operator. After off loading the operator insures that all hoses are emptied prior to disconnection. He then closes the receiving valve to insure that no further material may be off–loaded without approval. Vehicles containing bulk solids are directed to specific loading bays where materials are stored in covered buildings.

A similar procedure is followed for drummed wastes. After drums are moved to the storage area, each drum is labled with the information required for future processing. So you see, we leave nothing to chance."

"But how do we know some of the material won't leak out on the ground, contaminating our water supply?" asked another member of the audience. Now the speaker was warming up to the situation. He seldom looked at his sheet of typical questions and answers. The answers were on their way as soon as they were asked.

"The placement area where we put the Sealosafe product is monitored continuously. Any water coming in contact with the AntiPol product is collected and analyzed to insure it is free of contamination before discharge. And liquid collected from the placement area, which does not meet regulatory requirements, is treated. As final assurance that treatment and placement do not affect the groundwater, the entire site is surrounded by a series of monitoring wells. The results of these analyses are submitted to appropriate regulatory authorities. These authorities have access to the facility in accordance with regulatory requirements."

The questions kept coming but now they were repetitious. There were awkward pauses while the crowd sought to fill in gaps with their own comments. It was obvious they were not going to accept as full value everything the company shot at them. The format was to be underlying theme of many more confrontations between the company and the residents of Groveland Township.

Making sure that everyone had their say, Supervisor Titsworth ended the public comment saying that the company would have to file a Site Review Application before the Planning Commission, plus engineering drawings, after which according to State Act 64, the matter would have to come before a Site Review Board of nine members that decide environmental issues.

The meeting had ended but outside the township hall, little groups of people vented their angry feelings.

"You know what it's going to do to Groveland Township?" one man said. "We're going to be known as the biggest chemical dump in the U.S. Not only will they be hauling in wastes from Detroit, Flint, and Pontiac, but the whole Midwest region."

"Why do they bring it in here?" someone asked. Groveland is the center of state recreational areas. We've got the third largest ski lodge in the state, a country Boy Scout camp, and a County Park. Let 'em take it somewhere else."

Public reaction was high. The fight was far from over.

Phase II of the legal battle started one month later. The planning commission met and turned down AntiPol's application for a construction permit, citing violation of township zoning ordinances, violation of the usage portion of the Master Plan and lack of clarity about a proposed land reclamation plan that the company had submitted.

AntiPol, meanwhile, tired of behind the scenes maneuvering, took its battle to court. The legal expenses began to "burn" the township. It was David and Goliath all over again—the township with a budget just over $100,000 versus a multimillion–dollar corporation operating with unlimited money and resources.

Angry electors, seeking more money, petitioned for a special millage election to fund the extra heavy legal expenses. It passed by a huge margin.

# Chapter 13

When the third Site Review Board meeting convened two weeks later a new dimension was added. On the stage was a long table with a white paper tablecloth. The top was filled with a conglomeration of test tubes, Mercury Burners, mixing bowls, and scales.

It looked like a tenth grade Chemistry class was about to get underway.

Nearby was a man with a white lab coat, carefully measuring ingredients and making adjustments with scales. The crowd buzzed over the unique scene and wondered what was going on.

They didn't have long to wait. At promptly 7:30 p.m. Chairman Tierney gaveled the meeting to order. If anything unusual was in the wind, Tierney didn't indicate it. He was coldly insensitive to what was going on at the lab table.

"I have before me a special request from one of our board members, Mr. William Balloon, for a special report," the chairman said.

Balloon appeared briskly from the wings in his white lab coat. He was the Groveland Township member on the Site Review Board. He took a position in back of the lab table, moved it forward slightly so that people in the wings could see as well as those in dead center. Silently he flitted back and forth making last minute adjustments in his equipment while the crowd stirred uneasily, wondering what was coming.

He walked forward, center stage, placed his hands on the labels of his white lab coat like a chemistry professor about to deliver a lecture and said: "Ladies and Gentlemen. In the previous meetings you have listened to some highly technical talk about pollution and waste disposal. By a simple 10th grade experiment I am about to show you what happens when certain chemicals are mixed. These chemicals are the equivalent of the same kind of pollution AntiPol would be putting into the air over Groveland

Township if this firm locates here."

Saying that he donned a gas mask and prepared to go into his experiment. The mask would be alternately pulled up and down as he talked while the experiment progressed.

"I ask you not to worry about what will happen because you are far enough away from the experiment that you will not be bothered. Further, the amounts mixed are so small that they won't bother anyone. I only put on the facemask because the odor is rather smelly and an irritant. However, mixed in sufficient quantities what I am doing here could be very harmful to humans. I want the board to especially watch this experiment.

Balloon moved to the end of the table where a pair of surgical gloves had been carefully laid. Nonchalantly he picked up the gloves, pulled them on with considerable dexterity and aplomb. He looked like he had conducted this experiment a thousand times.

"The first ingredients I will mix are Hydrochloric Acid and Sodium Hydroxide, then in the next experiment I will mix Sodium Hydroxide and Sulfuric Acid."

The crowd tensed as Balloon prepared to mix the ingredients from the two test tubes. The buzz of conversation accelerated and spectators near the front frantically got up and moved as fast as they could to the back. The crowd tensed and a frightened look was in their eyes.

"Just a minute Mr. Balloon." It was the voice of Chairman Tierney speaking. "I'm afraid I will have to forbid you from making this experiment. I have a degree in Chemistry and I already know what the results will be. However, if any of the Board members wish to remain afterwards to watch what Mr. Balloon wants to do they may and I will have no objection. But for now let us go on with other deliberations."

Now the crowd noise was at bedlam level. There were shouts of, "Let him go on. We want to see what happens. We're the ones involved not you."

Tierney gaveled the meeting back to order. "Up to this point

the meetings have been quite orderly but if there are more distur-
bances in this auditorium I will by law close this session and we
will meet secretly. I have no other choice."

"If I am forbidden to proceed with my experiment may I at
least continue with my report," said Balloon. "I have other
information to impart even if my lab report doesn't go through."

"You may," Tierney said.

"Then I would like to point out the dangers of having one
building for acids and bases. If this project goes through, and I
sincerely hope that it doesn't, I would suggest that these chemical
units be separated in two buildings, at some distance apart. I would
also propose that the company should be forced to finance a
waterless fire fighting system. I hope, too, that they have stringent
provisions for spillages because if they happen you won't clean the
mess up with a mop and bucket. I would call this project a
400,000–ton experiment, because that's the amount of waste they
will be bringing into Groveland Township if they go into a three–
shift operation. And, one does not take lightly to putting a 400,000
ton experiment over a major water aquifer."

Concluding his report Balloon said: "The AntiPol product,
Sealosafe should be tested by the Department of Natural Resources in some isolated area, certainly not in a fast growing
township such as Groveland."

"The effect of Michigan's cold weather on the AntiPol product is unknown, especially in converting the Sealosafe process to
hard rock. 'It might not set for days.'"

"The 'scale–up' formula would be severely overtaxed. In
England, that plant processes 20,000 tons a year. That would mean
a scale up of 20 to 1 in Groveland. There would be no telling how
the system would work under that huge scale up. It might work
and it might not."

"The company has stated that it would only treat inorganic
wastes. Yet one of the wastes that would be processed would be
paint wastes and this is organic, not inorganic."

His report completed, Balloon took off his lab coat and resumed his seat with other board members.

# Chapter 14

A local environmental group was formed. They called themselves "Concerned Citizens of Groveland Township." They swung into action, scheduling a rally near I–75 and Grange Hall Road on a Saturday morning. The intersection was near an overpass of Interstate 75. Their strategy was to stage the rally in full view of hundreds of motorists traveling along the freeway.

My assignment for the day—cover the CCGT rally in Groveland Township.

It was an assignment of mystery.

What happens at an Environmental Rally, I wondered. I guessed there would be lots of signs and marches so I swung my Cannon AE1 around my neck, made sure I had a fresh battery pack and cleaned up the lens. I remembered back to that last time I used it, at a pig–wrestling contest in the mud in Ortonville. My picture unexpectedly came out with big blotches. A squealing pig, about to be wrestled to the turf, slurped a big glob of mud in my direction. I ducked, but a small piece hit my lens, an embarrassing situation. I had to explain what the blotch was in my cut line under the picture.

It was one of those moderate bright sunny days in Michigan, hardly a cloud in the sky.

The traffic along I–75 was heavy, many people fleeing the Detroit area for northern Michigan with thoughts of fishing, golfing, relaxing or camping on their mind. The lane hoppers were in their glory. They couldn't wait to whiz by the next car, darting between lanes like a space ship dodging asteroids on an electronic game machine. They might make it to their destination eight minutes earlier but the time factor made no difference. It was a game to them. Sometimes the game ended in death but that as a thing not to be looked at on a beautiful, bright, sunny day in Michigan.

I thought to myself—well, if the environmentalists want a full display of their rally they are going to get it today. Thousands of motorists would be driving by. It would be like a living billboard in 3–D.

I found it impossible to find a parking spot near the overpass. The area was thronged with cars. I heard a loud speaker system blasting in the background. I could just barely pick up the voice but it seemed like someone was giving instruction on how the rally would proceed.

As I climbed towards the overpass I spied a television crew on a nearby hill. They were trying to pick up a panoramic view of the marchers who were dressed in blue jeans and white T–shirts lettered with their favorite AntiPol slogan. The rough ground didn't bother the crew but the Anchorwoman was having a hard time. Her smart slacks had picked up an assortment of burrs during her climb to the top, and her fashion shoes had a thick covering of dust. The crewmen would probably have to photograph her from the waist up.

As I started my trek downward, after reaching the overpass, I came across an imposing scene of sound and sight. Over 300 marchers were scattered over a half–mile of roadway. In the background a combination of rock and country music was being piped from a van equipped with an overhead loud speaker. Rally leaders clutched BullHorns and gave their fellow demonstrators a continual series of "Pep Talks."

"Ladies and Gentlemen," the speaker said.

"We're not here to cause riots or start fights. We want a peaceful demonstration. Hold your signs up straight. Push them up and down occasionally for emphasis. Make sure they're aimed straight at the TV cameras when you see the cameras aimed in your direction. Don't smile when the camera focuses on you. This is a serious situation. It doesn't need smiles. Don't crowd around in the background when a newsman is interviewing. We want our message to get across straight, we don't need gawkers."

His message was heard but not seriously taken. Soon a crowd gathered behind a picketer as the cameras zoomed in. Some waved. Some edged between others so their faces would show.

Hucksters had invaded the rally and were selling balloons emblazoned with environmental slogans and making little animals dance on the end of a stick.

The Concerned Citizens, seeking to fortify their treasury so they could carry on the battle with AntiPol, manned a booth and were selling buttons, caps, pennants and other paraphernalia, all shouting anti AntiPol slogans.

I approached one of the marchers for a one–on–one interview. He was wearing a gas mask. Seeing the camera and notebook I carried he obligingly removed the gas mask to talk.

"Why the gas mask?" I asked.

"Well, that's what we're going to need if AntiPol comes in here. The air will be polluted with poisonous fumes."

"Aren't you jumping the gun a little bit?" I asked. "AntiPol says air and environment will be kept clean. They have an air filtration system ready and liners underneath the ground to catch spills."

"Listen, you and I know that's what they will do in the beginning, you know, to conform to state regulations. But a year or so down the line when all the fanfare dies down and they start making money they'll get sloppy and then we'll have another 'Love Canal'."

I looked at him. He was wearing blue jeans, sneakers and a white T–shirt that said "Groveland not Graveland." He looked just like an average American citizen, the kind that watches TV with a can of beer in his hands, plays with his kids, takes the family camping on weekends. What about all this stuff I had been reading about the 'silent majority', the kind that sits at home and grouses about issues but never takes a stand? He hardly looked like an activist, yet he was.

"What's your occupation?" I asked.

"I'm a tool and die tradesman in the GM plant at Pontiac."

"How come you got mixed up in the environment?"

"My wife and family moved over here to Groveland four years ago. We like the place. It's nice and clean; not a lot of people around and it has a rural atmosphere. We came here to get out of the city. Now all of this is going to change. Groveland is going to be the Chemical dumping ground of the Midwest."

"How do you know this AntiPol product won't work if it's given a chance?" I asked.

"It's possible. But why experiment with it in a nice clean, rural area like Groveland? Why don't they take it to northern Michigan where they've got a lot of space for that sort of thing."

"Maybe Northern Michigan wouldn't like that either." I said.

"You know what I mean, somewhere where they won't be surrounded by lakes, campgrounds and state parks, like here."

"Have you ever participated in rallies like this before?" I asked.

"No, I've stayed on low key pretty much but this is a very important issue to me and my family. In fact, I was one of those voting to levy special millage so we can fight this corporation. It's money out of my pocket but I don't regret it a bit."

With that he re–attached his mask and got back in line, saying "Sorry, I've got to get back to the picket line."

I moved on to another marcher.

He was a tall, gangly black youth, in his early twenties. I wondered what his reason for marching was.

"Can I talk to you a minute?" I asked.

"Yeah man, sure," he said. Gas mask removed he was ready for action.

"Where you from?"

"Whitfield."

"What are you doing in Groveland?"

"Hey man, we're just as much caught up in this as these people are." He waived his hand at the other marchers. "I've got a lot of buddies in this parade. If this company gets in, poisons our water, we'll be the next to get it. Our water table is right in line with theirs."

"You don't agree with this method of getting rid of waste, surrounding it with a rock–like material and burying it in the ground?" I asked.

"Hey man, cement cracks, don't it? I worked for a home-builder once, I know. What happens then? You've poisoned the ground, then whatta you going to do? It's too late then."

He moved back into the line of march. I turned to look at the signs the marchers were carrying. They were bold, colorful, and different. You could pick your style like picking cheese sharp, mild, or medium.

"Say yes to Michigan, No to AntiPol" read one sign. Two women dressed in white robes with faces painted chalk white carried a ghoulish sign "Doomed and Tombed with AntiPol." Something rustled between my legs and I looked down to see a little terrier carrying a black banner with white lettering reading "Stop AntiPol."

I needed one more interview, one where I could get the woman's slant, an equalizer to an already heavily weighted story dominated by males.

She was wearing blue jeans with a white T–shirt that read "Go Back to England, AntiPol." She was small, petite, and talking a mile a minute to a fellow marcher. She broke off as I approached notebook in hand.

"What brings you to Groveland?" I asked.

Her eyes flashed suddenly and she gave me a haughty look that made me wonder if she were an ERA (Equal Rights for Women) follower.

Right away she set me straight on that.

"It's not because of my sex, I'll tell you. My husband and I are in this thing up to here." She brought her hand up to her neck in emphasis.

"Then why?"

"Why? Because my husband is one of the Concerned Citizens leaders. We've spent every moment of our spare time checking on AntiPol. We've been down to the State Capitol twice and attended regional conferences on pollution."

"You don't think the system will work?"

"It's not all that. We've been checking on waste disposal companies already operating in Michigan. Do you know they're operating at only 65 percent of capacity? So, why do we need another waste disposal plant? What we have now is adequate."

"Are there other concerns you have about AntiPol locating here?"

"Yes. We're afraid of property values going down. We have a beautiful five–room house in the country. But we'll be near the AntiPol plant. Can you imagine what will happen to our property when they start bringing in all of those chemical trucks and burying all those wastes? Look. I know you're in the newspaper business and you're supposed to treat the news impartially but please be sure to get our side represented. Our only hope is to get this thing out before the public," she said.

I told her that I would but I also reminded her the system works two ways with each side getting equal time.

I learned later that AntiPol was calling a press conference the next day. Their chances would come.

I was about to leave when an interesting display caught my eye. There was no doubt it was intended for the press and a group of lensmen was already snapping pictures.

I waited until a press photographer from another paper finished shooting and stepped out of line. Then I moved forward with the Canon.

A ghoulish sight greeted me.

In front of me was a replica of an old fashioned graveyard with white slab markers pushing up from the ground. There were seven white tombstones plus a half–opened wooden casket.

All of the tombstones used one prevailing headline—"Rest in Peace, Our Air; Water, Rest in Peace:" and finally "Rest in Peace, our Campgrounds." Other carryover themes referred to contamination at Mt. Holly Ski Area, a local ski lodge that attracted skiers from all over Michigan, and a sign with a skull and crossbones reading "What if—" As I got ready to photograph the scene a group of people obligingly put on their gas masks and moved in back of the tombstones.

I saw some members of the Groveland Township Board. They would be good background color. I asked one of them what he thought of the rally. His was the typical comment you would expect from a political figure to give the press, guarded and people oriented.

It's not that their intentions were dishonest. I think they were being careful because of the previous lawsuit against the township clerk, based on comments she made during a press conference.

"Just great," he said. "What a fine outpouring of dedicated people, all coming forward to show others that we are determined to stand united."

"Do you think AntiPol will get the message?" I asked.

"How can they not help but get it," he answered. "We have three television stations here, plus four daily newspapers and the local weekly newspaper."

"What do you think will be their reaction?"

"Their reaction will probably be to dig in deeper. That's the discouraging thing about this issue. They have millions to spend. We have thousands. But we are determined and this crowd today shows you what I mean. But, it may be that our best game is to delay things awhile."

"What do you mean?"

"I mean this environmental issue is changing rapidly. What is legal today is illegal tomorrow. A new state law, Act 64, has just been enacted. Under that law a Site Review Board of nine members decides environmental issues like this."

"Will that help you?"

"It may and it may not. We will have some local representation on the board; hopefully we can sway a decision in our favor."

I thanked him and moved away, at the same time catching the eye of a Township Trustee on the Board.

"What do you think of this?" I asked. The noisy background of people who crowded in on us nearly blocked out his answer.

"It's stupendous. A great outpouring of emotion," he said. "Our board needed it."

"Why do you say that?"

"I mean some of us have been down in the dumps about fighting this issue. AntiPol seems to have endless amounts of money. We keep wondering if we are going to run out of funds and there is an attitude by a few people who keep saying 'give in they're going to win in the end, anyhow, why throw away township money?'

"How long do you think Groveland people will continue to support you?"

"As long as there is hope and as long as the appeal courts go along with us. But the money thing is frightful. Up to this point we have spent $150,000 for the battle. On the other hand, AntiPol expenses must be astronomical. They just paid out $5,000 for a one 10–minute documentary film on their English plant to show Judge Brakley."

In my notes I indicated that the rally was peaceful. The marchers shuffled back and forth along the road. There was shouting but no obscenities were heard nor were there any angry emotion outbursts. A State Police patrol car, engine cut off, was parked along the road but the patrolman inside looked like he was bored with the whole affair. He would carry out his assignment and make a routine report. And although the background was quiet the event would get its share of publicity on TV, the press, and radio. The citizens group was out for coverage, not violence. They wanted awareness and they would get it.

The rally was starting to break up. The marchers dwindled and displays were packed up to be ready for another rally. There was talk that the AntiPol people were thinking of constructing disposal sites in other states. In that case it was certain that regional rallies would be held. The sign makers would be busy. Some of the signs were destined for appearance in Ohio and Indiana.

An announcement was made that there would be a Country Western dance that night in Groveland, a fundraiser to replenish monies used for research studies, signs, and expenses. That night TV stations would air portions of the dance, as well as the daytime demonstrations. The marchers would see themselves on TV, the signs would be seen by half a million people in Southeastern Michigan. The battle was reaching its peak.

Over dinner that night at the old fashioned Whitfield Hotel I talked about the rally with my slim waisted brunette from Rochester. Over candlelight, a Prime Rib dinner, and the dusky smell of incense the time wasn't appropriate about talk of air pollution and industrial wastes but she injected it into the conversation anyhow. Her field was poisons and the matter interested her.

"I can't get over how dedicated these people are," I said. "Not only do they take tax money out of their pockets to fight the battle but they spend hundreds of hours volunteering on fundraising projects, doing research studies and making displays."

"Yes, and the news in the papers and on TV certainly have helped their cause," she said. "I can see why they're concerned. Look at Love Canal and those people in Texas where the government had to buy up their homes because of the Dioxin scare. It's horrible."

"I know they're concerned," I said. "But also look at it this way. Something has to be done about industrial waste disposal. It's a big, unsolved problem. You just can't go on putting the stuff in barrels and dumping it along the nearest country road. The country needs a proven method of getting rid of industrial poisons."

"No one knows more than I do about that," she said. "I heard you say you were attending a press conference by AntiPol, perhaps you will find out more about it then."

The waitress interrupted our thoughts with a dessert tray laden with Chocolate Mousse laced with whipped cream Banana Cream pudding and an assortment of little cakes. Pollution and the AntiPol company suddenly disappeared in delicious mouthfuls of rich Banana Cream pudding laced with mounds of fluffy whipped cream and petite cherry tarts. Just as suddenly my thoughts turned to more important things of the evening…a lovely face softly silhouetted by candlelight…a smile that lit up the corners of a pixie mouth…eyes that crinkled when she talked…a forehead that profiled the smallest worried thought.

Not only is this lady attractive, I thought, but she cares. She cares about people, the world, and the environment and maybe she cares a little about me. The thought added warmth to an already glow from the smooth, white wine. Our minds seemed entwined as one. It was an evening where thoughts stimulated thought, where ideals by one were magnified by the other, like an electronic sound ramped up a thousand times by a stereo amplifier; where 'body language' by one was adopted by the other; where minds transgressed bodies and met somewhere off in space.

It was time to leave. All of the dining guests had left some-time ago. We were alone. The candle was now a petite flame in a mound of yellow. There was restless activity in the kitchen, the banging of pots and pans, the sound of dishes being piled upon another, the scraping of food from the plates.

"I think they want us to leave," I said.

"They leave no doubt about that," she said. "It's been so nice the conversation, the wine, the food, the atmosphere. I almost hate to go."

"I do, too, but please add one more item to your list—you. I don't know when I've enjoyed an evening more."

As we rode home even the Mustang reacted to the magnetic

evening. Not even a backfire. Its rhythmic pulse was strong and the purr of the engine was like a healthy heart, beating, strong and vibrant. As we neared her apartment my arm left the steering wheel and found a responsive place around her shoulders. She nudged closer to me and as the car pulled to a stop I found her in my arms. Then came the tender words, the warm caresses spilling forth like honey on warm bread.

"You know," I said firmly, "we should see each other more often. I have a feeling we have much more in common then poisons and toxic wastes."

"I guess I feel that way, too," she said. "But I also want to help you in any way on the causes you are wrapped up with. The world needs answers. I hope you can find them."

"I'm going to try anyhow," I said.

All the way home I had had the feeling that somehow we were outward bound on a long journey towards truth, a journey that might wander into all kinds of interesting pathways. It would take common sense and intelligent thinking to separate the truth from falsehoods and rumors. There were lots of traps being set; it was up to me to avoid them.

# Chapter 15

The cry against the company continued to mount. On Environment Day CARE mounted a protest demonstration in front of the Whiteside Hotel where AntiPol was reportedly holding a strategy meeting on the upcoming site Review Board meetings. As leaders of the company entered the hotel signs waved excitedly and a TV newsman trailed one of the company executives into the hotel hoping for some off hand comments to feed a growing number of watchers who were suddenly interested in the "David and Goliath" story unwinding in Groveland Township. "Dooms Day is Near—AntiPol" read one dismal sign outside the hotel. "Go Back to England, AntiPol," read another. "AntiPol Guilty of Land Rape" was made like a streamer in a newspaper. Then picketing continued for an hour and then dropped off as the picketers scattered to their homes or jobs. The TV programs that evening would show blue jean clad picketers with anti AntiPol slogans.

My assignment for the day was to interview a company officer to "get the other side." Many of our stories so far were "anti AntiPol," except for the press conference, principally because they were images of public outcries. Now it was time to close the gap on pro sentiment.

After getting a few crowd shots I was planning to leave for other assignments in the area. I had planned to get back to the strategy conference right after its conclusions.

But before I left I was able to pick up on one of the picketers. He was a small man with a stubble of a beard dressed in the usual blue jeans with a T–shirt lettered "Bury AntiPol, not Wastes."

Seeing me he obligingly stepped out of line. The appeal of the press was working to magnificent perfection. It was amazing how a total stranger will become your warm friend once you have displayed the equipment of your profession, a pencil, notebook, and camera.

"Can I ask you why you are in the picket line today?" I said.

"You bet you can. I want a Groveland not Graveland," he said, repeating a phrase that was getting a lot of play as an Anti–AntiPol slogan.

"What makes you think it's going to be 'Graveland?"

"Because they're going to poison the land with hazardous wastes."

"According to the AntiPol Corporation that's not what they have in mind," I said. "They say their wastes will be pre–treated so when their product enters the soil there will be no pollution. They plan to reclaim it with Christmas trees."

"Christmas trees, huh, I guess they got you believing that crap, too. It's not the Christmas spirit they're interested in, it's money. First the wastes will come from Detroit, then Flint, Pontiac, Toledo, Fort Wayne and then the whole Middle West. They won't stop until they got us buried in wastes."

"Then you're saying you don't want them here, even if the product proves workable?"

"Yeah, we don't want them in here, period. And the product is far from workable. That film about their English plant proves that."

"Thank you for your comments," I said.

"Name's Rodriguez, R–o–d–r–i–g–u–e–z," he said. "Make sure you get it spelled right in the paper."

"I will." Inside I wondered if he was more interested in getting his name spelled right in the newspaper or whether he was really caught up in the cause. It would be interesting, I thought, to make an error in quoting him and then misspell his name and see which one he griped the most about.

After taking care of some routine assignments I returned to the hotel and saw men in blue and grey flannel suits coming out of the conference room. The strategy conference was over. Each carried attaché cases under their arms, some of the papers bulging out like an over–stuffed wastebasket. The typical executive look. It followed them like the label of a Campbell soup can. They were all talking and chattering at the same time, making motions with their hands to emphasize points, nodding their heads and catching their breath now and then as the pace of their talking and walking caught up with them.

"Pardon me," I broke into one conversation. "Could you direct me to Garrett Halderman, your public relations assistant?" I had read his name on the PR packet AntiPol had given the press at their press conference.

"He's just coming out of the doorway, the tall man dressed in the grey suit with the dark, straight black hair."

"Thank you."

I moved in his direction.

"Are you Mr. Halderman?" I asked.

Abruptly he turned towards me and cut short his conversation to devote his full attention to me. The pencil and notebook working its magical wonders, I thought.

"Yes I am. What can I do for you?" He asked.

"I'd like to talk to you about your strategy plotting conference," I said.

He was instantly on guard. I sensed disapproval of my choice of words.

"I wouldn't exactly call it a 'strategy plotting conference,'" he said. "We were planning on how to organize our case before the Site Review Board."

"Wouldn't you call that strategy plotting?" I asked.

"Maybe I'm looking at your choice of words in the wrong way," he said, "but in my mind if you're suggesting that we're hatching up devious ways and tricks to circumvent issues presented by our opponents you are entirely wrong."

"I didn't say that."

He thought on that, saw he was getting off on a rough start in an area that could cause his company irreparable harm. He countered on an apologetic note. "Excuse my clumsiness. I'm a little uptight about the demonstration, the picketing and such," he said.

"Could we sit down somewhere and talk?" I asked.

"Certainly, but where?"

"Perhaps we can talk better over a drink," I suggested. "How about that table over there." I pointed to a corner table in a secluded part of the lounge with lots of room to spread out papers and documents.

We sat down. The waitress in the pretty Martha Washington costume took our orders—Martinis, both with double orders of olives.

"At least we agree on our drinks," I said. "Somehow a talk about serious issues isn't right unless you can dawdle a bit with a olive on the far end of a toothpick and a Martini."

"In my profession, it sometimes helps to dawdle while you're thinking about an answer," he said.

"In mine, it helps to think about what the next question will be."

"And what is the 'next question?'"

"I haven't asked the first."

"Pardon me, go ahead. But before we start I would like to commend you for your courtesy and forthrightness. Too many of the media are on our backs. We are the people in the black hats, our opponents the ones with the white hats. We are the villains they are the heroes. We keep thinking that maybe the sides will change when the quarter ends but it never does. The game seems to be always fought in one direction only."

"I would like to ask you, Mr. Halderman…."

"Please call me Garrett."

"I'd like to ask you Garrett, how you can sit there and tell how you can be sure that this thing won't blow up in your face, like the most massive pollution accident in modern day history. Like an accidental spillage, an explosion, or a toxic waste pit like

'Love Canal.'"

"Well that's a very good question and one that we have done a great deal of research on. You know we're not just going to put our product in the ground. Each type of waste faces massive scrutiny, all kinds of checks and balances. And as far as the danger of an 'accident' that's about as remote a possibility as you can have."

"How can you say that?"

"We hired a traffic safety expert from Michigan State University to do a visual study of the Grange Hall area, where our new plant will be located. This guy has been involved in traffic and safety studies for 20 years, the last 11 on the faculty of Michigan State University."

"And what did he find?"

"Everything. There is less actual chance for an accident at this intersection because it is adjacent to a freeway (I–75) and most truck drivers on freeways are more careful and their trucks better maintained than on other roads. His study showed that the intersection could be the scene of a truck accident of this kind only once every 100 years or a hazardous waste spillage once every 212 years. He also compared accidents on the Grange Hall corridor for the past 3 1/2 years with the national average and found them lower."

"Okay, then what kind of Evacuation Plan do you have for this 'once in every 212 years accident.' You've already indicated that there can be one."

"There is no need for an evacuation plan. Since materials going to an AntiPol facility are not explosive, ignitable, fuming or malodorous, a spill will not result in a serious environmental accident."

"Well, what about accidental spillage? Even a small amount of spillage can be dangerous with hazardous chemicals."

"First of all, the transportation by truck to an industrial activity in itself, will be restricted to appropriate roads. Secondly the danger of an accident with a rupture of the container is practically negligible."

It was "dawdling time." Somehow the smooth, outpouring of stats and tables didn't fit all of the human elements, the fears, the frustrations, and deep–seated phobias that had everyone upset.

The olive did a flip–flop under the movement of my finger, like a cork popping up and down under the cautious nibbling of a curious fish. Absently I pondered the next question. Now it became a game. My game plan became to get under that smooth, unruffled public relations exterior. On the other hand he was trying desperately to keep it, to ward off the intruder who sought to invade his hemisphere. His game plan was to protect the company by words, by resource material, by statements or anything else he could get his hands on. You could compare his method to a skilled politician, answering questions from the press during a press conference. Oh yes, the questions were answered adroitly and glibly. But in the end was the question answered or merely detoured along another stretch of road?

"The Groveland Fire Department," I said, "is very concerned about spillages involving hydrogen and cyanide, producing deadly Hydrogen Cyanide gas. How serious is their concern?"

The answer came back fast and sure, like it came out of a textbook. He had studied his PR manual well.

"Such chemicals will be carried separately. There will be no mixing to get out of hand."

I probed further.

"The Groveland Fire Chief said his department would need $1.4 million to purchase suitable equipment to take care of hazardous waste spillage and accidental explosions, etc. He mentions a fire truck to fight hazardous waste spillage to cost $240,000; eight hazardous waste firemen's suits at $12,000 and even more."

This time it was his turn to dawdle. He didn't want to commit the company to expensive outlays for equipment. The olive got a bath and drying period at least five times before the answer came.

"Those are the figures of the Fire Chief. I have nothing to say either for or against them. However, AntiPol, for every emergency occurring in the community will meet such an emergency with a coordinated response with local authorities. This will include a fully trained AntiPol response team of AntiPol personnel.

Back to his dawdling he pondered a final statement, finally pumping his fist on the table for emphasis as the olive nearly did a half gainer out of his glass.

"Dumping of wastes without treatment has got to stop."

We now had consumed our drinks and the tip conscious waitress stopped by to inquire whether we wanted another.

"No thanks, I have my story," I said.

He looked at me evenly, without expression.

"I hope that I have been able to give you our side," he said. "AntiPol favors public participation in all of our operation. Industrial waste–treatment projects are often incorrectly perceived by the public and sometimes for good reasons. We do want and need public involvement in all of our operations."

The interview over I thanked him for his time. I left with a final request from him that our paper challenge questions from all sides of the issue.

I assured him that we would.

And now it was thinking time before the story made headlines.

"It's weird," I thought. "I've heard both sides and I still don't know who's right."

"But is that my job?" I thought.

# Chapter 16

The "Crazy Quilt" of legal moves droned on.

- AntiPol filed a reclamation site plan hoping to appease the Township whereby they would plant Christmas trees on the land when the disposal site had filled to capacity
- The District Court of Appeals ruled against AntiPol saying the company was in violation of Township zoning laws
- The Site Review Board, after several public hearings, denied AntiPol's application for site construction. The State Director of Natural Resources signed the official denial documents. His action was mandatory by state law if the permit application is rejected by the Site Approval Board
- The Township accused AntiPol of "scare tactics" saying AntiPol told them they would agree to drop the libel suit if the Township would sit down and debate the issues

There might be a place for AntiPol products in the future. Some felt the techniques could be there, if scientific testing could be done in isolated areas.

Everything was on wait now. Would AntiPol appeal the case to the Michigan Supreme Court? Would the Supreme Court accept the case?

As time went by the issue stalemated. The State Supreme Court decided it would not take the case. AntiPol gave up. They offered to sell all of their land for $10 to Groveland Township if Groveland would forgive all back taxes. Groveland accepted.

And that's how it all ended. A berm that was constructed to hide the plant from the public eye was to be leveled. AntiPol sold a new home that was to be the residence of the Waste Plant administrator. The end had come for AntiPol.

Time would tell who would win. The environmental calendar is ageless.

After my story on the AntiPol denial I had an easy day at the Herald. A feature story on area things to do at this time of year a couple of routine visits to the Sheriff's Department and State Police Post. Nothing exciting happening at either place. Routine stuff. And I was glad to get out of there at 5:00 p.m. quitting time.

It was one of those later summer afternoons in Michigan. Unbearably hot and steamy and pure torture for older type cars. I pulled up to the stoplight at Telegraph and Square Lake roads and the heat from the engine immediately stirred wavy patterns of pale smoke skyward. I looked at the engine temperature gauge and the needle was dangerously close to the "hot" marker.

Something had to be done immediately so I headed for Kris's apartment, not too far from my present location. While I heated up the Mustang could cool down with a cold drink of water.

I nursed the Mustang down Square Lake Road to I–75, took the south exit and headed for Rochester, hoping I could make it.

Kris's apartment was one of several complexes, nestled next to a private 18–hole golf course. It was unpretentious but clean and nice and in a good location.

By the time I arrived it was 5:30 P.M. Kris would be home by now.

I checked a dozen names before I spotted "Streeter" on the metal doorbell panel. I pushed the button and waited.

"Yes ."

A lovely vision of long, curled up legs on a davenport, dark soft hair and crinkly eyes floated down and out the speaker system. This time it had a drink in its hand.

"I'm wondering if you have started the 'Happy Hour' and whether you would let a hot, tired, frustrated newspaper reporter join you," I said. I intended to make the mood bright but it didn't seem to come out that way.

"If you're looking for brilliant, witty cocktail talk, go away. But if you want some solace for a rough, hard day come up and we'll knock heads together. I'm beat."

A buzzer sounded and the downstairs door opened easily under my push.

I knocked on the door and my lovely vision became reality.

"I think I might have to borrow some water, too," I said as I entered. "Mert, is also thirsty—and hot. Look I'm not busting in on anything am I? I mean if you have something planned I'll give my Mustang a drink and be on my way."

"I don't have anything planned and I'm glad you're here," she said. "But I'm not exactly the most charming host tonight. I feel pretty dull."

"I guess that puts us in the same class. It's been a frustrating day for me, too."

I then went into the Site Review Board's rulings, AntiPol's defiant denial, the balky Mustang, the rush hour traffic, finally getting to the feeling that I wanted to share some of my frustrations with someone I care about very much. I purposely low keyed the thirsty Mustang.

"Since we're both feeling in the 'pits' let's brighten things up a bit," she said. She moved to the stereo, put on some records and suddenly the room was filled with the soft, nostalgic music of "The Letterman," one of my favorite "groups."

"I know this isn't the total answer to our moods but it's a starter," she said.

She walked to the kitchen and soon there was the tinkling of ice tossed into a glass, the gurgling sound of liquid being poured from a bottle and finally the plop of an olive hitting gin. Ah, the sound of a Martini, I thought. You could almost build a symphony around it.

We sat around the cocktail table soothing each other's feelings. Each of us, we agreed, weren't responsible for the day's actions. She had had trouble calibrating a piece of faulty equipment for a Coma Panel. We agreed the Mustang problem was just old age and we settled on the AntiPol issue as just another part of a continuing drama. By the second Martini the mood had suddenly changed. The world was at fault, not us.

She had put a meat loaf in the oven, baked potatoes, and a salad. We moved from the cocktail table to the kitchen. She moved into a pretty bright yellow apron spotted with white flowers, donned colorful oven mittens, and gracefully removed the meat to the table. With a "Ta–Dah" and a flourish she set the table and lit two candles. We forgot the steamy world outside, settling on an orbit of inspired conversation, newfound intimacy and I felt a sudden awareness of her seductive charms. Our eyes met and we exchanged warm, intimate glances. We read each other's minds, saying things that we knew would make the other happy…we shared happy moments again, the first meeting, the dinner at the hotel, and now.

We finished the meal and she put on a fresh set of records. This time the mood changed. It was music with a savage thrust, "Light My Fire." We sat down on the davenport and suddenly we found ourselves in each other's arms, our bodies pulsating to the beat. Irresistible impulses set our heartbeats to a maddening pace. We were suddenly up and moving to the bedroom now lips and tongues meeting deliciously in long hot kisses all the way. Ours was a path of irresistible impulse. We were powerless to command our bodies. But as fiery as the moment was, it suddenly gave way to a cooler, more lasting, plausible, sensitive mood. It was unexplainable. One moment we were in a furnace, the next, in a "take it easy all the way" routine.

"You know, 'light my fire' is strictly a movie version of love. It's not my way," I said.

I looked at her. There was a dazed look of anticipation in her eyes where before there had been savagery.

"Not my way either," she said, slowly tousling my hair. "I

like a buildup not a fleeting second."

I went to the stereo and changed the record. The mood changed and the music slowed. Saxes and soft, muted trumpets filled the room. This time we could have been slow dancing in a small, intimate bar.

We looked at each other. Our lips met, cool, with a hint of delayed hotness. The buttons on her blouse parted silently under my touch, enticingly, one by one. The zippered slacks slipped smoothly from her hips as she laid backwards on the bed, her eyes in a hypnotic daze. Carefully, tantalizingly she unbuttoned my shirt, helped me as I carefully took off my slacks and slipped them on a chair.

Our hands were deliciously exploring, now, each touch sending shock waves of electricity through us. Our lips caressed each other's bodies in a dozen delightful areas. Moments later the entire universe opened up in savage ecstasy. Our pent up emotions released as two meteors meeting head on in space.

We broke away and lay silently for a few minutes.

"I suppose now, if we were in the movies, I'd light a cigarette," I said.

"We're not in the movies, Mike."

"Yeah, I know. The comparison was a bum one. I'm sorry."

"It's okay. I just have a feeling that perhaps we let things get out of hand. I mean the music, the drinks, the feelings and such."

"Are you sorry?"

"That depends, how do you feel?"

"I feel that I have just made love to the most loveable, the most desirable woman I ever met. Does that help?"

"Do you really mean that or are you just saying it to make me feel better? You could be a bastard, you know, and tell me the real truth."

"That IS the real truth, believe me."

"You're sure?"

"Absolutely, firmly and certainly."

Her hand slid to my chest. She was making little circular motions looking alternately up and down at me her eyes pouting and haughty, yet proud.

"I want you to know that this was a beautiful moment in my life," she said. "If I were to regret it I would have to turn off one of the most tender feelings I have ever experienced."

"I have the same feelings, too. It's too precious to do anything except take as a memory, to be recalled like a tape recorder of a beautiful moment in our lives."

"You have a beautiful, quaint way of expressing words, Mike."

"I don't mean too. It's the way I honestly feel, Kris. I wasn't trying to be expressive."

"I know you weren't."

"I have a feeling, Kris, that the evening was meant to start and end in this way, and this way only. I mean, my coming over, the way the car acted up close to your home, even the music, the drinks, the dinner, and other things. It was like it was meant to happen. Do you ever have the feeling that certain happenings in life, the timing, the pattern of things, bring about a chain reaction of things that you are almost powerless to control?"

"If you're referring to fate controlling our lives, no, I can't accept that. Life is what you make it."

"If life is what you make it, who or what puts thoughts in our heads, I mean, thoughts that end up eventually controlling your lives, your movements, your emotions?"

"I guess some higher intelligence."

"Then why can't you conceive that some higher intelligence can guide your life the way he wants to, set up moves and counter-move like a chess game, only the people involved wouldn't be just two people but millions…and the moves much more complicated."

"I never thought of it in that way, but, yes I guess he could. You've convinced me. Now can we change the subject? This is too worldly."

"Okay, let's talk about you and me. When can I see you, again, again and again?"

"On about the third 'again' you'll probably be tired of me. You're coming on pretty strong right now. Are you sure you wouldn't want to cool it for awhile?"

"I'm fond of you, Kris, terribly fond of you. If you don't let me see you again soon I'll think of a hundred excuses to land at your doorstep. Maybe a little more original, though, than the Mustang getting sick tonight. I'll hide behind one of your Coma Panel machines and grab you in my arms. I'll be a messenger boy when the next biopsy report is sent to your lab. I'll be in the back seat of your car when you start for home. I'll be the neighbor at your back door or the refrigerator repair man at your front door."

"Sorry, you don't fit in there anywhere. The management takes care of all the problems in the apartment. Don't have to lift a finger."

"Would you please get serious?"

"Sorry, I didn't know you wanted to get serious."

"I do. I love you Kris; I want to be in your life forever."

"Mike, I have a real feeling for you, it's something more than love, too, it's understanding, it's sharing of interests, it's what you call comparability, it's a lot of things. But understand we are both career people. We love our work. We are progressing in our fields, going to higher plateaus in our professions. Let's not get sidetracked for now. Let's enjoy each other, do silly little things together, go to the theater and plays and talk about them, cross country ski in the winter, water ski in the summer, take walks, have gourmet dinners at fine restaurants with good wine, even sit home and listen to records like we did tonight?"

"And make love?"

"And make love."

"What I mean is let's not wind up with snotty little kids with colds, nurseries, diapers and crying children in the night. I didn't go through six years of med school for all of that. It's not that I'm against it—in later years. But for now there's something much better, for both of us."

"I'm beginning to get the picture. You want a career, not a marriage."

"You're not getting the complete picture, Mike. You're only seeing the paint job, the outer skin, not the feelings inside. You have to look within. We can be happy, extremely happy in our work and in our love for each other. But let's leave out all the inconsistencies, the little irritations and frustrations of life. Let's go for the happy things, the things that tingle, the things that bring smiles, the things that laugh and sing. Tomorrow we can have all of the problems, meanwhile, let's live today. I guess I didn't mean to go melodramatic on you, I sort of got carried away."

"You put it well. I thought I was good with words. You're sensational. You could be a good newspaper reporter if you decided to get out of your field."

"Sorry, one is enough in my relationship. Now, can we get off the subject? Speaking of newspapers, what's new with you?"

I told her about the battle that just ended between AntiPol and the people, about the crisis regarding misinformation submitted in AntiPol's EPA application and some of my most inner thoughts on the issue. I told her the case was getting to me. I was getting involved where I shouldn't be. The people were closing in on me—so was AntiPol, it was time to assume my proper identity, that of a third party looking on.

"And how do you propose to do that?" she asked.

"I think I should shy away from the one on one stuff, the personal interviews, try to avoid the constant attempts by some people to influence my writing. I think I should attend more group meetings, get the feeling of the crowd, and keep hands off the personal stuff. If I look at it from the group standpoint I'll eliminate some of the froth on the beer, get down to the real stuff, and eliminate personal feelings. But it's hard," I told her, "I find myself being torn this way and that and people are sending out all kinds of hints, trying to find out how I really feel. I suppose if I was to do that, I mean let my feelings hang out, I could lay myself open to all kinds of influence peddling. I feel strong that I can keep an open mind if I really try, but I have to watch out constantly for traps."

"Now," I said, "tell me what's new in your business."

"Nothing much. Oh I forgot. I've been subpoenaed to appear as an expert witness in the Furman case. They want to know about the blood/alcohol tests I ran."

"Are you afraid?"

"I'm not afraid to stand on my ability. I guess, though, I'll be scared when they start cross–examining me. Some lawyers will try all kinds of tricks to get you confused."

"You'll be all right, you see, you'll be wonderful."

"I wish I had your confidence."

"Don't worry," I repeated, "you'll do all right."

I looked at my watch. It was near midnight. I had a story to write before the 10:30 a.m. deadline. I kissed her goodnight, took the open jar of water to satisfy "Mert," returned it after Mert had had her "nightcap."

My mind played havoc with me that night as I slept. Blue jean protestors were swarming around groundbreaking ceremonies for an AntiPol plant in Groveland. A bulldozer narrowly missed a couple of protestors and suddenly gunfire erupted. Strangely, I found my name on one of the protest banners. Then I was in a courtroom and Kris was being sworn in as a witness. She looked pale and white. I awoke when the Judge was gaveling the defense attorney down for shouting at Kris.

# Chapter 17

It was intermission time in a young reporter's life; time for a break; the third act was coming up.

The AntiPol issue was behind. Coming up was the Furman trial.

I needed something different, away from waste pollution, away from the scenario of a confused young man who wandered from a teenage drinking party to die a lonely death in a frozen cow pasture.

I needed to be by myself, yet I wanted to be surrounded by people. I didn't know what I wanted. Suddenly the earth, its people, the comedy of life, the tragedy of life, the loves, the hates, all was bearing down.

It was time for a change.

As an alumni of Michigan State I frequently found solace in the sounds of the gridiron; the bands, the people, the cheers, the groans, the thrill of rough contact on a field of green. It was a way to rid myself of complexes.

It was here, back to the big double decked stadium in East Lansing, that I decided to head on a bright, sunny autumn day; the trees in brilliant hues of yellow, red, and green. As I headed eastward I thought to myself there is no other place in the U.S.A. to be than Michigan in the fall.

In my own favorite spot is a high hill overlooking Herron Lake in the Whitfield State Recreation area. The view is breathtaking. You look down on Mother Nature's finest efforts. Her paintbrush is never better. Splashes of color are everywhere, even reflected in a clear, quiet lake. Outside of a church, this is probably the closest one can get to God. It takes you perhaps twenty minutes to get to the hill through winding curves alternately splashed with sunshine and deep shadows of green ferns. The ride escalates your emotions until they peak in a huge kaleidoscope as your car pulls into the scenic outpost.

Nostalgically I thought of that scene as the Mustang zipped along, the engine hitting smoothly on all six cylinders as the cold air gave it life.

My spirits were starting to peak, even as "Mert" slowed down to keep pace with the heightened traffic.

The cars were filled with fun–seeking people surrounded by picnic baskets, six packs and thermos jugs. That modern day innovation, "the Tail Gate Party," would soon spot the Spartan campus. The table cloths would be spread on make shift tables, the fried chicken would come out, the beer would flow and socializing would heighten as game time approached like a symphony tuning up for a concert. The buttons "Go Green" would make their appearance on green sweaters and the white MSU hats would hide balding heads of the alumni.

As cars passed it was fun to read the catchy slogans on green and white license plates. One, obviously in reference to the rival sister college of State read: "Michigan State, THE University of Michigan." This was the most hated license plate in Michigan by followers of the University of Michigan Wolverines. "Happiness, crushed Buckeye Nut," read another, obviously referring to the Ohio State Buckeyes, another rival of Michigan State Spartans.

Now the traffic was down to a standstill. Orange shirted security people waved frantically to clear bottlenecks but their assignment became almost impossible now as the game count down neared. The MSU band appeared and added to the problems. While they marched down the roadway a huge pileup of cars occurred to their rear.

I saw her standing in line at the stadium ticket booth.

I had one ticket to dispose of. Kris was indisposed that day; she had some drug tests to do—a hurry up job by the county, needed for court evidence the following week. I intended to turn back the ticket or sell it to someone in line.

The first thing that caught my eye was the hair. It was flame red and glistened as a bright sun beat down on it.

She was alone but it wasn't bothering her. She looked like the type that could be alone with a hundred people and not care a whit—although they might. I had a feeling that she could say a dozen words and get more attention than some witty, scatter-brained nut that talked chatterbox style for hours saying practically nothing.

The self–analysis ended as I approached. She was the last one in line and right in front of me.

I touched her and blue eyes with eyebrows the color of her hair stared back at me.

"I have a ticket for sale, would you like to buy it?" I asked.

She looked at me with a long, sidelong glance. It was a questioning look. She was apprehensive, up tight. I think she thought I might ask for a scalper's price. It was the Homecoming game with Purdue and the stands were almost a sell out.

"How much do you want for it?"

"The regular price, $12.00, no more."

Instantly the lines in the face relaxed. The apprehensive look melted.

"Fine. I'll take it."

"Just one more thing. The seat is in the upper stands. It's breezy up there and you might not like it—I thought I would tell you so you wouldn't be disappointed."

"That's just fine. That's where I sit anyhow. It's where I sat at the Notre Dame game. I find that when you sit in the upper stands you can see the formations better, the plays opening up, the line blocking and the receivers going down field better."

Her knowledge of the game amazed me. I'll bet when she was a young, towheaded youngster she caught more passes and scored more touchdowns than any guy on her block.

I handed her the ticket and said, "I'll see you there. I have the ticket next to you."

I began the long, slow tortuous journey to the top of the stadium. As an MSU freshman I used to make it topside in about three minutes. It was more like six now as age, lungs, and legs slowed by inactivity cut into my lifestyle.

She was already in her seat when I arrived at mine.

She was on her feet shouting "Yeah, Go State" as the pre–game ceremonies got underway and the Green and White marching band appeared in the tunnel at the north side of the stadium.

"Aren't they beautiful?" she said, motioning to the band and cupping her mouth so the words could be heard in the brisk wind.

"Yeah, they sure are," I said matter–of–factly. It wasn't the most profound statement of the day but I couldn't match her enthusiasm. I wonder if anyone could.

I looked at her youthful features. Everything about her physically matched her spirit, the alert, lively eyes, the laughing mouth, the cheeks that crinkled while she smiled, and yes, even freckles to match her hair.

She wore no lipstick—she didn't have to. She had such a healthy look that lipstick would only give her an air of artificiality.

Her face had the color of red leaves. She had all of the hardware of the All–American girl, I thought, and the spirit to match. Unlike many other women in the stands dressed in smart wool suits, she had a faded pair of blue jeans, a sloppy sweater and a three–quarter–length coat.

She talked constantly but sensibly. I found out that she was a 1980 graduate of Michigan State in Social Studies, supervised a school for retarded children in Mason, and was a resident of Troy.

I informed her that I had graduated in Journalism and we began a round of "Did you know who?" a fascinating game that usually took you nowhere because in a university of 41,000 students it would be amazing if you came up with even one mutual acquaintance.

Now the game was beginning and the chatter ended.

About midway in the first quarter she suddenly turned to me and said:

"Why don't they use Roberts?—he's the best runner we got."

I said I didn't know. He had been hurt earlier in the season but was reported to be just fine now. Perhaps he had a discipline problem with the Coach, I offered.

A little while later she said she was disappointed in State's game plan.

"Purdue is going to short pass State to death. They should spread the line backers, bring them up closer to the line."

Then she was bothered by referee calls.

"That wasn't pass interference. The Spartan guy was going for the ball. He has that right, you know."

I nodded absently, a thought occurring in the back of my mind that she must be going steady with a football player to get all of this background, or perhaps her father or brother was a football coach. There had to be some linkage.

Now she was sputtering unthinkable words about the referee, scolding him for what she said was his stupid unfairness.

"Yeah, Yeah, go back to the Bushes where you belong," she shouted.

Now there were grins on the faces of nearby fans. They had picked up on her spirit, talking, arguing, and agreeing with her on game plays.

And on it went.

She had the sports jargon of Howard Cosell and the intensity of a cub reporter at his first job.

I thought she would quiet down at half time.

She didn't.

When the Spartan band started to play variations on the hit musical "Annie" she was on her feet again.

"They're beautiful, they're really beautiful. Look at the way that drum major is strutting. His back is almost touching the ground."

As the game wore on it became increasingly painful that it

just was not MSU's day. The turnovers, the pass interceptions, the penalties, the fumbles took their toll and gave Purdue a 14–point lead.

But she didn't let down one bit. The words for the referee got stronger as the game neared its end, thankfully for State. Now she was shouting encouragement for the Spartans, shaking her finger at the referee, groaning at the mistakes and turnovers. She suffered agony when a Purdue lineman blocked an MSU kick, ecstasy when a Green and White running back sprinted for 23 yards.

And now the game was four minutes from the final gun. Die hard that I was I stuck around until the Spartans gave up the ball and had to punt.

I turned to her and said: "I'm leaving. It's no use, you know. There's no possible way for MSU to win."

She didn't say a word.

I walked to the aisle way along with hundreds of other fans that saw the futility of it all.

I looked around at her for a final remembrance.

She was on her feet shouting "C'mon State, give it to 'em."

I had a vision then of a daughter I hoped I might have some-time in the future.

She had red hair and eyebrows to match, a crinkly nose, a laughing mouth and freckles.

She knew what to do on third down and eight when a referee made a wrong call on pass interference and what a screen pass was. She liked kids, especially ones that weren't so fortunate in life; and she could curse with the best.

# Chapter 18

I was starting to get serious about Kris and maybe before the Furman Trial got underway, this was the time to do something about it.

I know that on the night we had made love we had taken an on–the–moment vow not to get serious with one another. But the scene had changed since then.

Now, I saw her everywhere in my imagination. Composing a news–story her face would appear at the end of a paragraph. Sometimes the face would reflect an impish smile as something funny struck her. Then a couple of paragraphs later her smile changed suddenly to a deadly serious frown as she contemplated a major roadblock in her never ending struggle to achieve success in her medical field.

Our moods became one. And, following a laugh we would embrace with a light, quick kiss, her face all crinkly and funny. Then in a serious moment our arms would entwine, our faces touch, like we were given each other assurances that everything would be okay in the end.

And sometime that light kiss would end up serious and passionate as our emotions intensified to a point where we would no longer control them.

It's time to get down to solid ground on this affair, I told myself. This can't go on. I want to be with her forever. Yes, marriage definitely is in the picture.

As I pondered the future I knew I had another step to take. Having been brought up in a laid–back conservative mid western family, that meant maybe it was time to bring her and my mother together and introduce them.

Old fashioned as the idea might seem to some, it was the "only proper thing to do" in my way of life.

My mother had lost her husband early in life. He had succumbed to colon cancer after a long, tortuous battle. She had kept faith with him throughout that battle but it was not to be.

Now she lived alone in a nondescript two–story white house across from the State Park entrance in Harrison.

Everyone in Harrison loved Ethel. Talkative and thoroughly outgoing she made friends easy. Loveable as she was, however, she developed eccentricities as some widows do after living alone, especially in Michigan during its long, winter months.

She made "friends" with local deer hunters who sold her venison out of season. She had a passion for picking wild mushrooms and knew all the select spots where they could be found. When asked where these spots could be found she shrugged her shoulders and said in a mysterious way "down along the railroad tracks."

When asked what railroad tracks and how far down did one have to go she shrugged again and repeated "down along the railroad tracks." Everyone gave up then.

She also loved to ice fish. When she sat down on her ice stool to fish Budd Lake that's all she had to do—sit.

Fisherman would spud her holes, leave her alone and then check on her periodically to make sure she was all right.

Kris and I arrived there in late afternoon on Friday. Ethel already had a pie in the oven and something on the top of the stove that was supposed to be pot roast but appeared wasted and slushy and immersed in a gravy that looked like a mud puddle.

Trying to work up an appetite on this mess was like looking down into you–know–what at the bottom of an outdoor privy.

We tried to eat with relish but ended up picking half–heartedly at what she had sat in front of us.

At the end of the meal we had left about half of the portions on the plate.

At that point Ethel picked up her fork and absently started to eat what was left on our plates. "I hate to leave anything on the plates," she said.

Kris was aghast. I was ashamed.

But the worst was yet to come.

Ethel remarked that she had some ice cream in the freezer that would "just hit it off" with the apple pie. She asked Kris to go down and get it out of the freezer.

Kris came back with the ice cream but halfway up the stairs she looked ashen.

"Guess what's in the freezer?" she whispered.

"What?" I said.

"A frozen blue bird."

I almost gagged but managed to gasp out, "Don't say anything, it's just one of mother's eccentric ways."

We left it at that. I never did find out what that frozen blue bird was doing in the freezer.

After dinner we adjourned to the living room. I had brought a tape recorder hoping to record mother's voice for a family album I was compiling.

"Mother," I said, "I am making a record of family members for an album. I would like to have you record your voice so we can all remember you by. Pick out something in your life that is treasurable, emotional, friendly and family."

"Yes," she said, "I have something to talk about that you can all remember me by."

She then took the microphone and told the filthiest, rawest, dirty joke that I have ever heard in my life.

At first Kris shrunk back in absolute shock.

Then she burst out in laughter that must have lasted two minutes.

"Are you sure that's what you want us to remember you by Mother?"

"Absolutely. Just don't tell that to your kids, if you have any, until they're of age," she said.

After the shock of that moment we talked family talk for about an hour and then I wanted to get Kris out of the house and into a more intimate, lively atmosphere.

I chose a bar that had always appealed to me when I used to visit my mother during my college years.

It was called "Muskie Pete's."

"Muskie Pete's" was what I always thought of as a "man's bar" although quite a few of its patrons were women who liked to go along with "their man's" male, macho image.

The Muskie part of the name originated because it lay on the fringes of a lake known to be the "best Muskie fishing in Clare County."

As you entered "Muskie Pete's" you were greeted by an array of pictures of grinning fisherman with catches of huge muskies. There were verifications by game wardens as to size, and signatures by witnesses attesting to "the true statements thereto."

These pictures lined the walls of a lobby leading to the bar. While you waited for the waitress to assign you to a table you could ogle and let out an occasional "wow" over one of the more spectacular catches of the day.

If you wanted to you could set yourself at the bar and wait for your waitress to yell at you because that was the only way you could be heard over the din of the television barking out their latest baseball scores.

The waitresses wore denim shorts and colorful T–shirts emblazoned with a picture of a large muskie and in print, "Muskie's Bar."

It was early evening and we chose adjoining bar stools. I listened while the jukebox played the latest rendition of James Taylor "You've got a friend." It blended obscenely with a summary replay of the Detroit Tigers–Toronto Blue Jay baseball game.

Dreamily, I thought about when "the guys" and I used to come in here after playing a night softball game, talking man talk, telling dirty jokes and bragging about the women we had seduced since last we met.

"What'll you have?" the waitress asked.

I bolted quickly out of my dream and said: "Martini on the Rocks," then adding "and fill it up to the top."

"Rum and Coke," said Kris.

We sat there juggling our drinks not saying much, but taking in the atmosphere and then, after what seemed only a moment in time, our waiter was telling us we could be seated.

I asked him to pick a quiet place, where we could talk.

He did.

Located at the far back of the bar it was screened by a large wooden enclosure with a lattice–like fringe upper cap.

The waiter took our order. This was not an upper class bar. He didn't have a black tie, a white shirt and tuxedo type vest. He wore blue jeans and had the already obvious "Muskie Pete's" T–shirt. But they were spotlessly clean.

Of course we both ordered the Muskie special.

We sat dawdling, wondering what to say in these surroundings.

Somehow, I felt philosophical.

I wanted to get my feelings out about Tommy's death.

Strangely, this seemed like the perfect place to do it. Drinking was going on, the room was filled with hilarity. But nothing unlawful was happening. People were being sociable, friendly, hardly obnoxious, and life was going on as normal, like it should be.

I found myself saying: "It shouldn't have happened."

"What?" Kris asked.

"Tommy's death."

"Why?"

"The reasons are obvious."

I went on. "Tommy Furman was just trying to be 'one of the boys.' How many times have you heard that phrase? Boys trying to be like men. They're not, you know, but they're trying to. A boy gets into a friendly father–son football game. The father tackles and pushes the son to the ground. The son gets up crying. The father says 'don't be a sissy' be a man."

Tommy's antics the night he died when he was trying to act like a man are almost a Mark Twain adventure where Mark pulled the old pillow under the bed routine. Just like Tommy did only Mark Twain's adventure turned out to be a folklore. Tommy's ended up in his death.

Mark Twain ended up living the life of a gangly immature youth on a riverboat. Tommy's life ended on a frozen cow pasture, after consuming a half–pint of Southern Comfort.

Tommy's dilemma started when he got drunk and started to vomit. Not liking to clutter up a clean house Tommy was taken outside and dumped. How come no one took the time to sober him up and put him in a place where he couldn't harm himself?

And where were all the adults at this time?

One was in a room watching television.

How come the adult wasn't out checking on the kids to see that they were behaving?

I remember my graduation party. My mother was checking on things happening upstairs. My dad was checking on things downstairs. Once in a while they would change places to get different viewpoints.

When Tommy's body was found it was thought he had lain out in the cow pasture 12 to 14 hours before he died of exposure. Why wasn't he missed? How come no one checked up on him after he disappeared from the party?

Those who absolve the people who hosted the party said too much happened between the time that the booze was purchased, consumed, and the death to accuse the two people charged with involuntary manslaughter.

I don't think so.

It should have been apparent to someone, either adults or teenagers, that Tommy was headed for disaster.

Tommy's mother wants the guilty parties to be held account-able. She thinks a guilty verdict could be a deterrent to future wild–youth parties that end in death.

She wants a mature adult to call parents when their son or daughter is too drunk to ascertain what is right or wrong.

She would like the callers to identify themselves and then state specifically: "Your son is drunk, please come get him."

If they don't, what's to prevent that drunken person from getting into a car, driving away from the party, and hurting, maybe killing an innocent person?

She doesn't want another Tommy Furman ending up in a frozen cow pasture.

Who knows the agony Tommy went through as he passed into oblivion? Did he suffer? They say when you freeze to death you slowly sink into unconsciousness. The half–pint of Southern Comfort must have lulled him into a state where he could do nothing to help himself.

What a way to die. Just lay there unable to move, unable to signal for any help, even though you wanted to.

Tommy's blood level at the time of his death was near .07. That's not being legally drunk, but the medical examiner says if he was alive in the field as long as he thinks he was, his blood level could have been three times that when he left the party.

Why didn't someone notice that?

"Why didn't they?"

The case was getting to me.

I probably wouldn't sleep that night.

Kris was feeling it too.

She was teary–eyed. She put her hand on my shoulder, trying to console me.

I looked up at her. I think she understood what I was going through.

Looking back, I later thought maybe a bar wasn't the proper place to express your feelings on Tommy's death.

But then, what was?

# Chapter 19

The courtroom was crowded with people as Judge Alice Elkins, clad in traditional black robe, swished elegantly to her seat and stood absently surveying the audience. The case of People versus Robert S. Conley and James W. Hunter was about to begin.

"Hear yea, Hear yea," the court recorder sang out. "The Circuit Court for the County of Oakland is now in session. Please take your seats."

The toiling of the press was evident. The case had been played up prominently not only in the *Oakland Herald* but also most of the Detroit area media.

The Detroit Free Press and Detroit News, engaged in a death struggle for circulation gains and both anxious to pick up additional subscribers in the Oakland County area, had sent reporters to the trial. An artist from a Detroit area television station stood poised with a sketching pencil and pad. The good Judge's countenance would be etched before 25 million people on the late evening news that night. She stared blankly ahead, however, oblivious to the attention of the media. Not so the court recorder. She noticeably primed her lips and slid her hands down the lines of her trim dress, smoothing out last minute wrinkles. As the artist turned around to look at the audience smiles suddenly broke out.

The clerk sang out: "The People versus Robert S. Conley and James W. Hunter. The charge, Involuntary Manslaughter."

"Please swear the jurors for examination on the voir dire," the Judge said.

The court clerk faced all the jurors and raised her right hand.

"You do solemnly swear that you will true answers make to such questions as may be put to you touching upon your competency to sit as jurors in this cause, so help you God."

Obediently, all the jurors answered "I do" and sat down.

"Please call a jury of fourteen," the Judge ordered of the

clerk.

The clerk reached into a square wooden box containing slips bearing names of each member of the jury panel. Then he slid open a panel, and conscious that all eyes were upon him, pulled out a small paper slip with a flourish that like an Arthur Murray instructor demonstrating how to do the "Hustle."

Each name on the slip was called out with a relish approaching an actor on the stage delivering lines from Romeo and Juliet. When the nine men and five women had been pulled, Judge Elkins picked up the information sheet supplied by the People and read: "The People charge Robert S. Conley and James W. Hunter with willful adult negligence in the death of Thomas Furman. The charge is that the deceased attended a teenage party at the home of James W. Hunter where alcoholic beverages were illegally given to minors and that Thomas Furman wandered away from the party intoxicated, to die in a field from exposure. They charge Robert S. Conley with furnishing liquor to Thomas Furman that later resulted in his death from exposure."

"Now ladies and gentlemen," said Judge Elkins, "I am going to examine you to determine if you qualify to sit as jurors in this case. Even though I may not address you individually, I expect you to speak up if any of the information I give you pertains to you. Please raise you right hand if you wish to respond. And remember you are all under oath. Do you understand this?"

All jurors nodded their head 'yes' and Judge Elkins droned monotonously on.

The judge then explained the obligation under criminal law of determining guilt beyond a shadow of doubt and presumed innocence until proven guilty.

All understood the instructions and dutifully nodded their heads yes. Then Judge Elkins went on to the statutory qualifications.

"Are you all citizens?" she asked. "Raise your hand if you are not."

Again no show of hands.

Then the routine questioning began. Were any of them deaf or in poor health and wish to be excused; were any over 70 years of age; did all of them speak and understand English; had any prospective juror served on a jury in the circuit court in the last 12 months; were any governmental or state or municipal employees and wish to be excused; were any of them law enforcement officers and were any of them related to the defendants.

All answers in the negative.

"I shall now pass on to examining you for cause. The Prosecuting Attorney, Mr. Pillister, is sitting at the right of counsel's table. Are any of you acquainted with him."

Some raised their hands.

"I will not ask you if any of you know him intimately?"

The hands remained in place.

"Do any of you have any pending business with him and do any of you know of any reason or situation that you have come in contact with him that would in any manner prevent you from deciding this case freely and squarely on the law and evidence presented?"

Silence, no dissent.

"Now, let's go to the defendants, Mr. Conley and Mr. Hunter, seated at counsel's table to your right. Do any of you know them?"

Again silence.

"Finally, we go to the deceased, Thomas Furman and his family. Do you know any members seated in this court, or out of court?"

"I do, your honor," a thin faced man about 50 answered.

"Who do you know?"

"My daughter knows Tommy Furman. He had been at our house a few times."

"What is your name?"

"Gerald Jolly."

"Mr. Jolly, was your daughter at the party at Twin Oaks?"

"Yes sir."

The Judge motioned the Prosecutor and the Defense Attorney to the bench. A hurried conference ensued.

"You will be excused, Mr. Jolly. Please step down."

The prospective juror sighed contentedly. He looked like the type that didn't want to get involved.

The clerk went back to his box and pulled out another slip. This time the prospect made it all the way through the questioning.

The People had 15 peremptory challenges and the defense 20. Under peremptory a witness could be dismissed with a wave of the hand. Finally, after all of the peremptory challenges had been made a jury had to make it through challenges for "cause."

It took two peremptory challenges and three challenges for cause before the Furman jury was picked. After being sworn in, the jury was ready for the opening day. Their number would be pared to 12 before going for deliberations on a verdict.

"You will present yourselves in this courtroom next Monday at 9:30 a.m. sharp for trial. In the meantime please do not discuss this case among yourselves, or with others. If any person tries to discuss this case with you, please report it to me at once," said Judge Elkins.

"Hear yea, Hear yea," the clerk sang out. "This honorable court is adjourned until 9:30 a.m. Monday."

"Jury Chosen for Furman Trial" read next day's headline in the *Oakland Herald.*

The case got full play in the Detroit media. It was expected. The Anchorwoman on the 11 o'clock TV news held an artist's sketch of a smiling judge, the two defendants and a prim court clerk. Comments on how swiftly the jury had been chosen were sprinkled with comments from the audience reactions.

Outside the courtroom the TV people had tried to interview the defendants on their way out to waiting cars but they brushed aside the questions with "No Comment." Interviews with the

Prosecuting Attorney and Defense Counsel, however, were published or aired in carefully couched remarks. Each side was confident of victory.

Tommy's mother had sat silent in the front row. She looked straight at the defendants continually without expression. It was a scene that would be repeated each day of the trial.

After the jury was selected the courtroom emptied fast. I sat in silence studying my notes.

The silence was eerie but I welcomed the chance to collect my thoughts.

In the next few days, I thought; a decision of far reaching importance would be made. What had the prosecutor said—"A Landmark Case." It was a heady feeling that I would be in a front row seat, getting a first hand look at a moment in history. It was a little bit scary, too, a sense not only of duty but heavy responsibility.

# Chapter 20

The trial got under way with opening statements by the Prosecutor and Defense Counsel. It was clear that neither was going to go with their best shots at this stage. Better to wait until the end, leaving the jury with peaked emotions just before they made up their minds.

The Prosecuting Attorney's statement was concise and to the point: "We will prove that Thomas Furman became intoxicated to the point of insensibility, that he wandered away from a teenage drinking party at Twin Oaks Ranch, and, unable to help himself, fell down in a field and died of exposure. His death was directly caused by the two defendants, one of whom supplied him with liquor and the other failing to take action in a life threatening situation."

Counsel for the defense said neither of the defendants was responsible for Tommy's death, that there were too many intervening factors and too many adults at the party to put the blame on just two people. It was a record that would be played many times before the trial ended.

The stage was being set for a battle of keen, legal minds that would go down many pathways, take bizarre twists and change dramatically the lives of two people.

I looked at the defense attorney. I had heard that he had a lucrative practice in the nearby city of Bloomfield Hills, catering to the rich and near rich. As a partner in the law firm of McKinnon and Hatcher, Robert Hatcher was said to have a smooth manner, a hair trigger mind and an expert in what football jargon is known as the "trap" play, a favorite ploy of the legal profession where a witness is unwittingly led on to admit several transgressions, then "trapped" by their own testimony.

A six footer in his early 40's he had the physical stature of a tailback, and according to my sources the cunning of a quarterback. Good looking, he adroitly had his hair cut in moderately conservative fashion, pleasing both those with old fashioned tastes and his contemporary clients. His Bill Blass dark blue single–breasted suit fitted him perfectly, the white cuff on his shirt protruding correctly 1/4 inch from his coat sleeve. A judge would find it difficult to pin a label on him. Women jurors would fall in love with him.

There was no doubt how you would assess Prosecutor William Pillister. A young man in his late twenties, he had a flowing black beard, hair combed straight back, and intense, no–nonsense manner. I had known William Pillister for two years. In that time he had acquired a reputation for preparing "tight" cases for the Prosecutor's office, leaving nothing to chance. His research was faultless although his delivery lacked the drama, the excitement, and the emotion that goes with a successful trial lawyer. He was thorough, relentless, concise, and dogmatic. He told me he hated the "fluff" in the law, the courtroom drama, the unexpected, the bizarre, the flare. He was a devotee of the law, the whole law and nothing but the law. There would be no nonsense in his presentation, only the facts, ma'am.

Judge Elkin gave instructions for the Prosecutor to present the first witness.

Carole Lansing, a mother of one of the youthful partygoers at Twin Oaks, approached the witness stand. She was a plain, wispy woman, thin with heavy wrinkles lining her face. She looked tired and beat down.

"You do solemnly swear that you will tell the truth, the whole truth, and nothing but the truth, so help you God?" said the clerk. The question was posed in sing–song fashion like an eighth grader reciting lines at a church Christmas pageant, probably due, no doubt that it had been recited hundreds of times in the past to a point where the words were meaningless, the thoughts empty.

"I do."

"Please state your name."

"Carole Lansing."

"Will you please tell the court what happened between you and your daughter on February 21, 1981?"

"Well, we were in the living room of our house discussing the party at Twin Oaks Ranch. My daughter asked me if I would help her to have a keg party for her boyfriend, get the booze and stuff. I heard it was his birthday and they wanted a big celebration. But I wouldn't have anything to do with it."

"Objection!"

The voice, smooth and vibrant, came from the other side of the courtroom by the defense counsel.

"Hearsay evidence at second hand, consisting of testimony based on information that a witness has obtained from another person, not from first hand knowledge. What daughter said is hearsay."

Round one was underway. It had started like a prizefight with the combatants testing each other for strengths and weaknesses. A probe was underway right now. The upper cuts would come later.

Judge Elkins was on the spot. She knew it. The trial had barely got under way and she was being tested. She was ready. The objection had barely been sounded when the answer was on its way.

"According to my legal knowledge the hearsay rule applies to statements made for the purpose of medical treatment or medical diagnosis, recorded recollections, records or regularly conducted activities. But nowhere does it say requests or questions. The witness may continue."

"I told her I wouldn't lift a finger for such a party. I knew it was illegal and I didn't want her to get involved."

Under Pillister's expert guidance she then related that she found out later that her daughter, in company with Conley, went to a liquor store in Grand Blanc, where beer was purchased along with a pint of Southern Comfort for Tommy Furman.

In cross–examination Hatcher tried unsuccessfully to inject a pattern of conspiracy to obstruct justice.

"Did you," he said, "ever get instructions from Detective Fred Hansard not to talk to the defense lawyers?"

"He said I was not to be intimidated by them, that I should tell the truth and not be afraid, that's all."

"Did you get instructions from anyone else, any law enforcement person not to talk to defense counsel?"

She shook her head, no.

The court clerk broke into the conversation.

"The witness will have to say either yes or no because this is being taped. I can't explain it on the taping system that she shook her head and the tape won't indicate which way she's thinking."

"I would ask you," Judge Elkins said, "to speak clearly and concisely. Because this is being taped you must answer yes or no and not indicate your answer by shaking your head. Is that understood?"

"Yes your Honor."

The questioning continued.

"Did you know Mr. Hunter, the man whose house was used for the teenage party involving your daughter, the deceased and other teenagers?"

"Yes, I knew him."

"How well?"

"He was a good friend, a very good friend."

"When you found out about your daughter, that she had helped purchase some liquor at a party store and that she might be attending a wild drinking party that night involving teenagers did you get in touch with Mr. Hunter and tell him what kind of party it was going to be?"

"Objection!" roared the defense. "Excuse me, your honor, but I think it's crucial in terms of my client and his rights that strict rules of evidence be adhered. And I will note a very strong objection to a controversial line of questioning in a leading and suggestive nature by the Prosecuting Attorney. I do know that the Prosecuting Attorney has interviewed all of the witnesses. They're well aware, I won't say coached, but they're well aware of the situation is, as is the prosecution. My client's right is prejudiced by candid testimony which would occur if leading questioning is continued about what type of party is involved; certainly a designation of such a party as a 'wild party.'"

"Objection sustained. You will refrain, Mr. Pillister, from making referrals as to what type of party was taking place."

"Okay, I'll rephrase my question. Now, Mrs. Lansing, think carefully, I would like to refresh your memory about the party, where it was going to be held, what type of refreshments would be served, and so forth."

"I can't remember exactly. I'm a little bit vague on that."

"But don't you remember...."

"Objection!" the smooth voice of the defense counsel again. "My recollection of evidence law indicates you can refresh a recollection from cold fish to a newspaper. But the next question is does this refresh her recollection. And if the response is in the negative and you're fishing her out for your own benefit, that cuts out that line and you move on because now you're arguing with the witness. She said, no, it didn't refresh her recollection and that's it."

The legal harangue was now beginning to get to Pillister. The quiet, unassuming exterior disappeared in a blaze of anger: "Your honor, if my learned counsel will please shut up and sit down, I'll move on to some other line of questioning. I'm getting tired of all of his objections and we haven't even been into the first 30 minutes of this trial."

Judge Elkins gave both attorneys a long, unforgiving look. Finally she summoned both attorneys to the bench.

She spoke in hushed tones but her voice was firm, demanding.

"If we have any more outbursts in this courtroom like this,

you will both face censure, especially you, Mr. Pillister. You should know better. I will remind you that this is a court of law not a 10 round heavyweight fight. You will both conduct yourselves in dignified fashion or we'll adjourn this case and you'll both face legal action."

Both lawyers muttered timid "Yes, your Honor," the judge hunched her shoulders, gave a last glaring look at both and the trial resumed. The interview continued as she recalled incidents prior to the party—nothing shaking—nothing new. Then the prosecution was ready for the next witness.

"The People call Dr. Robert Spiegle," called out the prosecutor.

Dr. Spiegle, looking owlish in his large, horn–rimmed spectacles, approached the witness chair and was promptly sworn in.

After giving his name and a long list of credentials, the Oakland County Medical Examiner relaxed in his chair, his long, thin face in a contemplating mood as he waited the first question.

"Dr. Spiegle please explain what your duties as a Medical Examiner in Oakland County encompass." The young prosecutor was anxious to get on with the case but he wasn't forgetting the basics. He was packaging the product, but the paper, the string, the folding, all had to be neatly taken care of before mailing.

"As Medical Examiner of Oakland County, our office is called upon to investigate all deaths which are due to homicide, suicide, accident of any type, persons dying in police custody, persons dying as a result of therapeutic misadventures, persons dying without medical attention within 48 hours of their death, persons dying as a result of abortion and any death which is reported to be suspicious in nature. It is a statutory requirement that the Medical Examiner investigates these deaths and determines cause and manner of death, and during the course of the investigation he may perform an autopsy.

"Can you approximate how many autopsies you have performed during your tenure as Oakland County Medical Examiner?"

"About 10,000."

"And during your long career as a Medical Examiner plus your distinguished background as a graduate of the Villanova, Long Island College of Medicine, rotating internship at U.S. Public Service Hospital, Staten Island, resident and research fellow at National Institute of Health in Bethesda, Maryland, in Pathology and resident in Pathology at U.S. Public Health Services in New Orleans...."

"Objection! We have already gone over the good doctor's so–called distinguished record in medicine when he was first sworn in. There is no point in belaboring the issue. We're all aware that Dr. Spiegle is a distinguished man of letters in his field. So why are we building him up by re–emphasizing points already in the record? The Prosecution is deliberately trying to influence the jury through double emphasis."

"Your point is well taken Counselor. Please, Mr. Pillister get down to business and eliminate the fluff."

"Yes sir, I was only trying to point out Dr. Spiegle's distinguishing career in medicine."

"Get on with the questioning."

"Okay, doctor, please, could you give us a definition of Pathology?"

Definitions were right up the doctor's alley. He could reel them off like a scholar reading from Webster's Dictionary. No blurbs, no bungled words, no hidden meanings, it was all there in his mind, like pushing the button on a computer.

He drew himself up straight, looked thoughtfully out into the courtroom, flung his voice to every corner.

"Pathology is the Branch of Natural Science which deals with the diagnosis of disease through the examination of body tissue, fluids and the performance of autopsies."

"Doctor, I direct your attention to the date of February 26, 1981, and ask you if you performed an autopsy on the body of

Thomas J. Furman."

"Yes sir, at the Medical Examiner's office, 1200 North Telegraph Road."

"And doctor, prior to a body being examined at the Medical Examiner's office, between the time it is accepted and examined does your office go through a procedure as to what is done with the body?"

"Yes sir, the routine procedure in the matter is when…."

A roll of thunder echoed across the courtroom; the sound was akin to the violence of a storm, when the air is sultry and first rumblings are heard.

"Objection!"

This time the defense counsel was on his feet, papers in hand, a pointed finger gesticulating in mid air.

"Prosecution is trying to confuse the issue again. The most relative thing, I think, is what was done with this body, not what was routine procedure."

"May it please the court," said Pillister, "I was trying to get to this part when I was rudely interrupted by the defense counsel. If I keep getting these interruptions the Prosecution may never get its case in."

Judge Elkins: "If routine procedure describes what was done with this particular body, I will take that as proper testimony. Please continue with your questioning, Mr. Pillister."

"Your honor," said Pillister, "I'm relying on the rules—habit or routine practice is permissible to establish in evidence that at a certain time and a certain place something was done in conformance with habit and routine practice."

"I have already ruled on that, Mr. Pillister, please continue with your questioning."

His cause upheld Dr. Spiegle went through the routine procedures performed including tagging and refrigerating the body, the various pathological tests made and the final act, the autopsy. He repeated his opinion that death was caused by exposure to the

154

elements brought on by ethanol ingestion.

The direct examination over, it was time for cross–examination by the defense.

The doctor tensed as the first question hit. It was a natural reaction, a reaction of wonderment; what strategy was unfolding; the fear of being played the fool before a courtroom of people. The doctor, however, was reacting well; his body stiffened, his eyes took on a keenness like a Golden Retriever poised ready to flush a covey of Partridge. He looked into his interrogator's eyes. What he couldn't envision, however, was a surprise the defense had planned; a line of questioning that would later turn the courtroom into a frenzy.

The defense counsel walked nonchalantly and slowly to the witness stand, a pencil in his hand and a legal pad ready to take notes. He gave the witness plenty of time to stew and ponder the next move, a deliberate ploy to upset the doctor's dogmatic attitude.

"Now doctor, after conducting an external examination you testified that you performed an autopsy and examined internal organs including the brain. And after that you determined that the deceased died of exposure brought on by ethanol ingestion."

"That is right, sir."

"And in forming that opinion, what did you use for a basis?"

"My observations of the body, my experience and training and results of the tests that were given to me."

"Were these done by your assistant, Dr. Robert Jenkins?"

"Most were done by him, but we had some flooding in the lab at that time and we sent some of the tests out to a Medical Science Laboratory."

"Where did you look over these tests, were they on a report, on record, documented?"

"They were on a Toxicology report. That's a standard form used in a Medical Examiner's office where appears the name of the deceased, the various samples that were analyzed and the results of these analyses. The name of my assistant, Dr. Jenkins, appears at the bottom of the report and a rubber stamp of his signature."

"Your Honor," said Hatcher, "at this time I would like to strike Dr. Spiegle's remarks about the cause of death. He admits that his opinion was based on reports submitted by Dr. Jenkins and yet Dr. Jenkins is not in this courtroom to testify on his report. Once again we are into the area of Hearsay and inadmissible evidence."

Judge Elkins: "The court finds that if this evidence is to be admitted it must be admitted as the work product of Dr. Jenkins who is not here. Either the prosecution must produce Dr. Jenkins today or at sometime in the future where he can take the oath and be sworn in. Back to you Mr. Pillister."

The "bomb" was about to explode. It came later as Hatcher stalked his witness in cross. He was grilling Spiegle about his credentials when he suddenly shot at him:

"Dr. Spiegle are you presently at this time the Medical Examiner for Oakland County?"

"Yes sir."

"And is that pursuant to a court order that you're allowed to continue that position at this time?"

The doctor was taken by surprise. His shoulders suddenly slumped and he stammered.

"I–I–I refuse to answer that question on grounds that it might incriminate me. That case is now in the courts. You'll have to wait until the court makes a determination for your answer."

"Dr. Spiegle is it true that you were involved in a civil action where you determined that the cause of death in a person was an overdose of Valium and that under re–autopsy it was found that the Pericardium was never opened and that the cause of death was a massive Pulmonary Embolism?"

"Your honor," said Hatcher, "civil suit or not, Dr. Spiegle was allowed to say that in his opinion the cause of Tommy

Furman's death was due to ethanol ingestion. He testified that he signed the death certificate to that effect. It is now established, or at least confirmed by an evidentiary hearing that the people's witness is incompetent. I would move that his testimony be stricken from the record. Further, in evidence, I submit the following article in a local daily newspaper that at an evidentiary hearing these findings of incompetency were found to be substantially true."

Pillister stirred uneasily. A counter move was necessary quickly if the prosecution was to keep the integrity of the witness. He jumped to his feet, saying: "I find the defense counsel's remarks to be off beat considering he is basing his conclusion on a newspaper article. I have often been quoted, and wrongly I might state, in the newspapers. You can't make a conclusion out of this. He still has his day in court coming. At this time I would like to have Dr. Spiegle acknowledged as an expert witness in spite of the defense's unethical remarks."

"Gentlemen," said Judge Elkins, "we have reached a standstill in this case. I find it difficult to judge the competency of the witness but I find that his testimony is important. I will take his testimony pending further evidence of competency but in the meantime time is growing late."

Judge Elkins looked at her watch.

"It is now nearly 5:00 p.m. I am calling this case to a conclusion today, to be resumed tomorrow with Dr. Spiegle on the stand."

The long, first day was over. The jury was taken to a nearby motel and ordered not to discuss the case among themselves or with anyone else. There were too many diversions to say who had won the opening round. But Dr. Spiegle's credibility as a witness had suddenly been shaken. He would be allowed to testify but how important would that testimony be now? It was clear the prosecution would have to come up with another expert witness to maintain its credibility.

But who?

Although his testimony was now construed as "tainted," Dr. Spiegle the next day related how he theorized young Furman died of exposure, the lividity theory, the metabolism of alcohol by the body, the blood/alcohol tests, that there were no other intrinsic diseases present that could cause his death besides exposure to the elements and ingestion of alcohol. There were strong objections from the defense that Spiegle's testimony be stricken until his assistant appearing as a witness could substantiate some of the tests.

As the trial continued, other witnesses gave testimony and a lull then occurred as the Prosecution pondered its next strategy.

Then, from Pillister came a surprise statement, at least it was to me.

"The People call Kristin Streeter."

The name startled me. I had not seen Kris in the back of the courtroom, but then I'd been channeling all my energies into taking notes.

She was dressed in a plain double–breasted suit with large, flared lapels underneath a lacey white blouse. In the fashion of the day the dress just broke under the kneecaps revealing long, shapely legs that she crossed as she took the witness stand after being sworn in. She seemed cool, collected and confident, even under the glare of the defense counsel who seemed determined to stare her down.

The assistant prosecutor approached her and made with the usual amenities and small talk to calm her down. It wasn't necessary, however. She spoke without tremor, calm and confident.

After the usual rundown on age, address, etc. she went through her background as a Medical Technician; BS from University of Michigan; Medical Technologist for 14 years, worked for Providence Hospital for five years in the east, where she was supervisor of the Hematology Department, Massachusetts

Stoughton Memorial Hospital and University of Michigan Hospital at Ann Arbor.

With the ever–present pencil and legal pad the assistant prosecutor began the questioning.

"On February 26, 1981, did you receive a sample by courier from the Oakland County Medical Examiner's office, purporting to be that of Thomas Furman and bearing...."

The voice of the defense counsel broke in.

"At this time I would wish an opportunity to voir dire the witness as to foundation material that she might have had that she will be using to testify, so that we will at least have an opportunity to look at it."

"Do the People have any objection?" said Judge Elkins.

"We have no objection providing that the defense doesn't stray from the voir dire."

"All right then," said Judge Elkins. "Let us proceed."

The attorney for the defense approached the stand. He remarked that the witness had an unusually fine background in medical technology and that he in no way wished to question her qualifications. It was the usual "bedside manner" to put the witness in a cooperative mood. The move had no visible effect, however. Kris stared straight ahead, aloof to praise, or criticism for that matter.

"I see you have something in your hand. What is it?" said defense counsel.

"It is a copy and original work sheets and requests that come in with the specimens that we were asked to make tests on."

"Do you have any independent recollection of performing tests on the deceased's specimens, Thomas Furman?"

"No, I do not."

"In other words you get hundreds of these things coming in."

"Yes we do."

"What were the tests you were asked to do?"

"We were asked to do a Coma Panel."

"Coma Panel—is that done on a machine?"

"It's done on a variety of machines and by several different methods. A Coma Panel stands for Comprehensive Drug Screening. It's a screen that detects 40 different drugs in serum, urine and gastric juices. It involves performing anywhere up to 10 to 12 different essays. All of the drugs are not going to be detected by one instrument. I may have to use five or six instruments to confirm what I have found."

"Are you mad at me?"

The question was sudden, electric. Kris had answered the questions matter–of–factly, and without emotion. The question came from left field, sudden, upsetting. She was taken by surprise but recovered quickly.

"Not at all. I just wish to answer your questions."

"All right, let's skip that part and go on. Could you tell me what, if anything, could affect the validity of the test results?"

"Objection," said Pillister. "I thought the voir dire was concerned about her qualifications. There's nothing been asked about that. What is the defense trying to do, mask the trial in confusion?"

There was momentary silence. The Judge pondered her answer; then gave in a firm, deliberate voice: "It's the Coma Panel and the various kinds of machines that I don't know about. I'll take an answer to clear up the issue."

"In any analysis there is always the possibility of error," the witness stated. "There could be an instrument problem or error. There could be a reagent error."

"What is a reagent?"

"Reagents are substances that are used to detect the presence of other substances by the chemical reactions they cause. In other words when you take a specimen of blood or urine or bile or gastric material you have to put it with certain materials, depending on what we are testing for."

"If the Reagent is not either sterile or sound or pure or as it ought to be, then that could affect the validity of the testing?"

"It definitely is a possibility depending upon the test."

"Do you use Reagents when testing with the Coma Panel to determine the presence of alcohol?"

"We use an internal standards which you could consider a Reagent. When you deal with Gas Chromatography, which is the way we analyze for ethanol, the ideal way to perform it is to put in internal standards that you can measure the retention against that internal standard to determine the presence of the drug that you're looking for and so the accuracy of that particular test would depend upon the accuracy of the internal standard against which you have measured."

"So, if these materials are impure and inaccurate, this could affect the test results. Please answer yes or no."

It was the oldest trick in the legal book, 'answer yes or no' to get an answer favorable to your cause without discussion that would be unfavorable and a yes answer was almost a certainty.

"Well, I don't want to give you a yes answer or a no answer. There's more to it than that."

"Your Honor," said the prosecution. "The witness is allowed to qualify her answer if a complicated, technical issue is at stake."

"Yes, Mr. Pillister, I am aware of that," said Judge Elkins. "Is it possible for the witness to say yes or no and go on to qualify it?"

Defense: "Whatever, go ahead if you wish."

"I would say yes to your question but I would like to qualify it."

Defense: "Okay, now when you say you use an internal standard...."

Prosecution: "Objection. You're cutting the witness off. She indicated she wanted to give a qualified answer."

Judge Elkins: "The witness may go ahead with her qualified answer."

"I have to assume that the standards are what they're supposed to be and they are functioning. However to be sure I run a series of known standards, which give me results that I know, are dependable. In this case one of the standards was an in–house standard containing various volatile substances, one was a commercial substance that we get from a commercial laboratory in a sealed container. By running them through the gas chromatography machine I was testing both my known sample and my unknown sample. If they did not come out the way they were supposed to, then I would know there was something wrong with that particular Reagent or standard for control. And I might add those test results have to be within reasonable tolerances."

"What are the standards of variations that you consider acceptable?"

"We accept our volatility on the March standard—10 percent—10 percent of the stated value which in this case is two percent. If there is any discrepancy in the tests it would have to be the performance of the machine."

"And the performance of the machine could affect a greater spread of plus or minus ten percent if that machine is not calibrated?"

"Not if the controls came in as I explained. This is our allowable tolerance. And if this did not agree, we run a series of controls. And if we did not agree then we would not accept the run, we would not accept an answer."

"I would like to call your attention to a sample you received on February 26, 1981, purporting to be a sample of the deceased, Tommy Furman, marked autopsy number 108. Do you recall receiving the sample and performing tests on it?"

"I remember the number and description of the tests to be run, not necessarily the name. The description was of a 15–year–old male. We were asked to do a urine and blood sample test."

"Were you asked to do a Coma Panel?"

"Yes."

"Anything else?"

"We did a volatile analysis. We inject the specimen directly into a gas chromatography machine and look for the presence of ethanol methanol, isopropanol or acetone."

"Are these volatile substances?"

"Yes they are."

"Is it possible to have a volatile substance in the urine and not in the blood stream?"

"Yes, depending upon how much is present. It may be below the level of deductibility in one or the other."

"Did you test for any other material in the blood other than materials that are, or substances that are volatile?"

"No, I did not in this case."

"And just so we understand, when you test for a substance that is volatile you are testing for a substance which because of its chemical make–up emits a vapor. Is that the definition of volatility?"

"I do not know the definition of volatility."

"And you've been in this business for how long?"

"I've been a medical technician for 14 years. I can tell, you however, the volatiles that we test for."

"When you performed your tests on the blood and urine is it not a fact that you were only testing for the presence of volatile substances?"

"Absolutely not. I just explained that I tested for about 50 different drugs."

"Okay, I'll take your word. Now, did you test for any so–called street drugs, Mescaline, Marijuana, LSD?"

"We do not test for Marijuana or LSD."

"Are there so–called street drugs which could be evidenced upon analysis of bile or gastric juices and not evidenced by the blood and urine tests?"

"I really don't know about bile."

"You're not a 'bile woman' than?"

"No."

"With the exception of testing for ethanol or ethyl alcohol, what were the results of the tests for all other substances that you tested for?"

"There was nothing else detected."

"I have nothing more for this witness. Over to you Mr. Pillister."

"Can you tell me what happened in your testing of sample number 108, the Tommy Furman sample," said Pillister.

"I took the sample and injected it in the gas chromatograph. I got a peak corresponding to ethanol."

"Did you get an ethanol measurement?"

"I got a percentage of ethanol."

"Based on these calculations, first for urine, what was the blood alcohol of this sample?"

"We do not quantitate alcohol in urine. We don't feel that you can get an accurate quantitum off the alcohol."

"All right, what was the blood alcohol percentage of the blood sample?"

".074 percent by volume."

"Does this percentage indicate an intoxication level?"

"That depends upon several factors, the amount of greasy food in the stomach, the physical condition, etc. That is something a court of law is involved with. Under Michigan law, however, a person is considered too intoxicated to drive with a blood level percentage of .10."

"That is all I have for the witness, your Honor."

"You may step down, Miss Streeter," said Judge Elkins.

Kris had done well under cross–examination. She had not blanched fidgeted or wilted under the insistent prodding of Hatcher. If at all she had taken the defense aback with her direct, simple answers to highly technical questions.

# Chapter 21

The trial began to wind down and the Prosecution decided to eliminate some of the "side dishes" and get down to the "meat and potatoes" of it all.

Pillister stood up and in a rather stern and emphatic voice called out: "Your Honor, the prosecution at this time wishes to call Oakland County Detective Sgt. Fred Hansard to the stand."

Sgt. Hansard, I knew wouldn't be badgered by either of the two attorneys. I knew from background that he would give a cold, scientific account of the death of Tommy Furman. With all of the bookish theories, circumstantial evidence and emotional rather than local testimony offered to this point, his would be a refreshing addition to the trial.

"Sgt. Hansard," Pillister began, "please recount for the court if you will, the events that happened on February 21, 1981, relative to your investigation of the Furman death."

"Our office was contacted about a missing persons report from Mr. and Mrs. Furman. We went to the location to investigate. We set up a canine search for a Thomas Furman, a 15–year–old white male subject. I went to one area, my associate; Deputy James Pallard went to another. A short time later he contacted me by radio saying he had found something. We found the body laying one quarter mile south of the Twin Oaks farm, in a field approximately one fourth mile north of Belford Road."

"Sergeant, I've laid a pile of photographs in front of you, 26 in total numbers 26 through 51 as the People's exhibit. I'm going to ask you whether they are a true, accurate representation of what you know to be facts, as photographed, concerning the Furman case."

Hansard picked up the photographs and studied them for a full minute before replying.

"They are."

The accurate, scientific detective that he was, Sgt. Hansard matter–of–factly described each photograph like a doctor explaining an operation to his fellow practitioners in a balcony filled operating room.

"This picture was taken from the west, shooting in a north-easterly direction; number 35 was taken after the body was rolled over. It is a facial front shot. Picture number 37 shows the left sock with the pant leg being raised to indicate there were no shoes on the body when found. Picture number 39 shows the garments being down below the buttocks. Number 40 shows the scratches on the lower back just above the underwear shorts. Number 45 is a photograph of the pasture and the remaining cows at Twin Oaks. We used a tape measure to measure the wire weaving on the fence. It was a farm fence and the strands are wrapped. We wanted to get the width of the wire wrapping on the top strand."

"And what was the purpose of that?"

"There were marks identified earlier on the back of the victim that I had photographed earlier and they were approximately the same width as the fence. I requested a photograph to compare them with the width of the marks on the small of the back of the victim."

"And how did the widths compare?"

"I can't say exactly, but to me they appear to be similar. The fence at that point is a standard farm fence and it was bent over as if it had been crossed from east to west by something that had pushed it down."

"And where is that location in relation to the shoes that were found?"

"Directly over."

"Is there any way from your examination that you could form an opinion as to how recently the fence would have been bent?"

"There's a barbed wire strand that runs across the top that was rusty. The rust had been removed off of some of the barbwire just recently. You could tell that by looking at it."

"How could you tell?"

"The rust on the front of the fence had...you could...show that it had been there for some time. There were two barbs that showed they had been rubbed smooth. This would have had to be done in a recent period."

"Why is that?"

"Because the rust would have reformed on the barbs had it not just been wiped off."

"So, Sgt. Hansard, with all of these factors that you have given us, would you please give us your expert theory as to how Tommy Furman's body got to the place where it was found."

"Yes sir. It is my opinion that Tommy Furman wandered away from the party in an alcoholic state. Somewhere in the back of his mind he had intentions of going home. He followed the fence row for direction, climbed over the fence at this one point, lost his shoes in climbing over and shortly afterwards dozed off and died of exposure."

"Thank you. Over to you Mr. Hatcher for cross."

"Sgt. Hansard. Did you notice any livestock in the area where Tommy Furman was found?"

"There were some, yes."

"Is there anyway of determining whether a bend in the fence could have been caused by an animal; any way of making a distinction there?"

"There is no way of knowing that but I do know the animals were quite some distance from where the body was found."

"Did you attempt to discover the presence of any fingerprints on the body or on the clothes?"

"That's not my field, sir, but why should we? There was no evidence of foul play."

"Did you not consider the presence of scratch marks on the lower back, the bruised lip and the clothes being pulled down over the buttocks as worth of investigation?"

"The Medical Examiner's office indicated that the scratch marks had been caused by moving the body. We felt they had been caused when the victim went over the fence. We felt the bruise was not significant to have caused the death in itself."

"Your remarks about fingerprints not being your field did not answer my question to you sir, and may I say your statements about foul play I don't agree with and I consider them for what they are, theory not substantiated by facts. But let me rephrase the question. To your knowledge did you or anyone connected with the Sheriff's Department examine the body for fingerprints?"

"No sir."

"Thank you."

Finished with the witness, Hatcher quickly grabbed his legal pad and addressing Judge Elkins while periodically glancing at his notes said: "Your Honor, at this time the prosecution has concluded its case and I see not one iota of evidence, only speculation, as to how Thomas Furman got from a prone position of being asleep or unconscious at 2:00 a.m. at the rear door on an asphalt sidewalk where he was carried hand and foot, bodily dumped there and then ended up in a field when he was unable to walk by himself. How did he mysteriously get over this fence with no shoes on and his pants pulled down over his buttocks, with a bloody smashed lip, when he did not have those physical findings when he was last seen? We've had all of these kids in here testifying and the Prosecution tried very hard to shake them down, even when they knew there were a number of intervening causes that led to Tommy's death besides alcohol. Your Honor, I would like to make a motion that there has been no cause of death established, in other words, the corpus delicti has not been established which is required in a case where the death is of non obvious means, not like a gunshot or knife wound or something else. Second of all, in the Root case, People verses Thomas Root, it was established that intervening causes were a factor and in this case we have a number of intervening causes, causes subsequent to Mr. Conley's alleged purchase or assistance in purchasing and delivery of alcoholic beverages to the party at Twin Oaks. That makes the causation to be due to some other person, either the contributing negligence of Mr. Furman or the fact that he was physically removed to the outside from the bathroom into the cold elements of a February evening by two young people. Had he been left in the bathroom to sleep it off he would have had nothing more than a hangover for his bad habit instead of facing death in a field. Robert S. Conley did not put him in his elements. Mike Bettsler and Gerald Sommers put him into the elements. So how did he get to—how the deceased wound up in the pasture is absolute speculation. Was he carried there? Why did he have a 'fat lip?" Did he have a concussion? Did someone strike him and then did he succumb to the elements? All of these are intervening causes and smack with the Root decision. Judge Elkins—you have to dismiss the charge, that, one, the corpus delicti rule has not been established and, number two, causation has not been shown to be proximate."

Face flushed, Pillister angrily met the challenge.

"Your Honor," he said. "The prosecution would argue against dismissal because of the expert testimony about the blood–alcohol content in the body; we've shown that the deceased was furnished a pint of 100 proof Southern Comfort that helped lead, in our belief, to Tommy's death. We've established by evidence that the host for the party, Mr. Hunter, did at one point in the party go out and bring more beer into the house, that the amount of alcohol and beer consumed by the deceased would have resulted in his death because he was unable to care for himself in frozen temperatures. All of this that the defense calls 'intervening causes' definitely establishes guilt and this trial should continue."

The time of decision was here. The courtroom hushed. Only the ruffling of papers marred the silence. It took about a minute before a careful, deliberate Judge Elkins, staring out in space, finally rendered her decision.

"I do find here several intervening causes of death but both on the part of the prosecution and the defense," she said. "The party the night before I'm still convinced could have put him in a weakened condition, in spite of testimony offered otherwise. The possible carrying of Mr. Furman to the pasture offers another theory. All of these could have been intervening causes. And here we have the prosecution pointing to a blood/alcohol content of .07 and to say that was a cause of death. Absent something else, I've seen hundreds of people come into my courtroom in the high 20's of blood/alcohol readings. And yet, there has been firm proof of alcoholic beverage being furnished by adults at the party, there has been evidence of wrongdoing on the part of adults and there has been a lack of responsibility indicated where there should have been responsibility. I don't think Mr. Furman died from the consumption of alcoholic beverages but on the other hand that could have led to his demise. I would deny the dismissal so let's get on with things."

"Your Honor," said Hatcher, "since you have negated my request for dismissal the defense stands ready to present its case. I would like to call two witnesses for the defense, Don McKay and Dawn Roberts. Since they are both students at Whitfield High, we have obtained special permission from school authorities so that they can be excused from their classes while they testify."

"Proceed, Mr. Hatcher."

"I call Don McKay to the stand."

After the usual swearing in and routine questions concerning name, age and address, Hatcher asked: "I would like to refer to past testimony on your part when you were asked about being in the company of Dan Stocker and he told about Mike Dooley and his girlfriend putting Tommy in the pick up truck of Robert Hunter, and driving around with Tommy in the back of the truck. I have the testimony of Dan Stocker right here and he said he did not talk to you about this incident. Now I am going to ask that question of this witness and it is regarding the same subject. 'Did you have any conversation with Dan Stocker and what was it?'"

"Objection," said Pillister. "This is hearsay evidence. It's a statement not admissible under the Michigan rules of evidence. Besides, this would not prove that he actually did drive him around, or what."

"Objection sustained. Please rephrase the question or discontinue it."

"Okay. Did Mr. Stocker ever tell you, in the presence of a number of other people, that Mike Dooley and his girlfriend put Tommy Furman in the back of Robert Hunter's pick up truck late on the night of the Twin Oaks party and then later went for a ride with Tommy Furman in the back of the truck and that at one point during the ride they stopped and noticed that Tommy was not in the truck any longer?"

"Objection, the question has been rephrased but it still carries the same meaning."

"Your Honor," said Hatcher, "this question does not fall within the definition of Hearsay evidence. We're not trying to prove that Mr. Furman went for a ride in the back of the pick up truck, or anybody else's truck for that matter, just whether this was said."

"In that case I'll take an answer."

"The answer is that yes he did state that to me and my girlfriend."

"Are you sure he said that?"

"Yeah, I'm sure."

"Did Robert Hunter have a pickup truck on February 21, 1981?"

"I believe it was his. I ain't sure if it was his or not."

"Okay, I have no further questions. I would now like to call Dawn Roberts to the stand."

Dawn was a shy girl in her middle teens. She fidgeted with her hair constantly, her eyes darted every which way and her hands were always in motion. Her sentences rambled and it took two or three questions to get any meaning from her answers.

"You were friends with Thomas Furman, were you not?" said Hatcher.

"Yeah, we were good friends. I'm pretty sure, anyhow."

"Did you occasionally drink with Tommy?"

"Yeah, we hit on one or two or three, I'm pretty sure."

"How often did you drink with him?"

"About once or twice every two weeks he would sneak something from his home and we would go out to the barn or out under a tree, or something. I'm pretty sure."

"Your Honor the prosecution respectfully requests that the witness give direct answers to the questions. When she says she's pretty sure, nobody knows whether she means yes or no."

"Miss Roberts," said Judge Elkins, "I would ask you that when you answer future questions you either indicate that you know for sure an answer or that you say 'I don't know,' is that clear?"

"Yes your Honor."

"Okay. Now, Miss Roberts on those occasions that you drank with Tommy Furman would he get drunk?"

"Yes, sometimes."

"How drunk—answer me on a scale of 1 to 10."

"I would say about five or six."

"Based on your contact with Mr. Furman was he a regular drinker about five or six months before the party?"

"Yes."

"And did you tell the investigating officer of the Sheriff's Department that Tommy would drink what he could wherever he could get it?"

"No, I did not."

"Were you at the Clark Gas Station in Grand Blanc on February 25, 1981 where Dan Stocker worked?"

"Yes."

"Who was with you when you were at the gas station?"

"Don McKay."

"Did you have a conversation with Dan Stocker when the name of Tommy Furman was mentioned after Tommy's body had been discovered?"

"Yes, that was the talk of the town, then."

"Did he make any statement to you?"

"He told us that he knew that Mike Dooley and his girlfriend put Tommy in the back of the pick up truck, went for a ride, and when he stopped the tailgate was down and the kid was gone."

"Thank you. Over to you, Mr. Pillister."

That was it. Somebody was lying but whom? It would be hard to prove. One person's words against two others. The assistant prosecutor approached the witness, a serious look on his face.

"Miss Stocker, do you know the penalty of perjury, that you could be sent to jail if you falsify a statement under oath in this court. Are you aware of this?"

"I am."

"And you still insist that your answer is true?"

"Yes."

"That is all I have for this witness. The Court will note a discrepancy in testimony between three witnesses. Without knowing all the facts the jury will have to decide which story to accept, unless it wishes to subpoena the other witness and bring him back on the witness stand."

Looking at her watch Judge Elkins noted it was close to the noon hour. She ordered that the jurors be taken to lunch and that the trial resumes at 2:00 p.m.

I had a few questions to ask the defense attorney. They were routine questions and when I finished I picked up my notebook and prepared to leave. As we were about to part he startled me, saying: "Stick around friend for this afternoon's session. You're going to hear something that will knock your hat off."

"What's it about?"

"I'm sorry but I can't tell you."

With that he stuffed all of his papers in a brief case, consulted briefly with Judge Elkins and strode out of the courtroom.

I could hardly wait for the afternoon session. What was the 'knock your hat off' bit all about? I bolted my food down and found I had 45 minutes to kill. All kinds of twists and turns had surfaced in this trial. What possibly else could be unleashed? My mind was racing in all directions like buckshot from a .12 gauge shotgun when Judge Elkins gaveled the court to open at exactly 2:00 p.m.

"Mr. Hatcher, I understand you have more defense witnesses to present."

"Yes, your Honor, I would like to call John Walkinshaw to the stand."

If John Walkinshaw were the witness that was going to 'knock my hat off' he didn't look it. Of slender build, thin face, nervous walk and manner, he looked like the timid soul right out of the cartoon series. I'd bet a dollar that as a youth he muffed his lines in the church Christmas pageant. He acted like the worst place in the world he wanted to be was on the witness stand. He fidgeted and squirmed and stretched his neck several times trying to relieve his stress.

"Mr. Walkinshaw how long have you been a resident of this area?"

"About two years. But I was born and raised in Oakland County."

"Where are you employed?"

"I am employed as an electrician for GM Parts in Drayton Plains."

"Did you place a call to one of my clients, Robert S. Conley, recently?"

"Yes I did."

"Do you know Mr. Conley personally?"

"No, I just saw him for the first time in this courtroom."

"Did any person from his family contact you prior to the time you placed the telephone call?"

"I didn't even know he existed."

"Have you ever had any contact with me or any member of my firm or did we ever represent you or any member of your family in a court case?"

"No."

"What was the nature of your call to Mr. Conley?"

"I read about his involvement with the law in an area newspaper. I saw he had a problem and so I called him. His name was in the newspaper so I looked it up in the phone book and called him. I had read about the boy's death in the paper but at the time it didn't appear that Mr. Conley was involved. Later I read where they placed charges against him."

"What did you tell Mr. Conley in your call?"

"I told him I had talked to the boy the night that he died on a CB radio and I didn't know if it would be useful to him or anyone and if it was, why Okay I would be available."

"Now, after you talked to Mr. Conley did he refer you to me?"

"Yes."

"And we spoke and subsequently I interviewed you at my office?"

"Yes."

"And you're appearing here pursuant to a subpoena I served on you?"

"That is correct."

"I would direct your attention to approximately 11:00 p.m. or 11:30 p.m. on the night of February 21. Could you tell the Court where you were at that point in time?"

"We were traveling on Interstate 75 approximately one mile north of Whitfield Road, when it started."

"What started?"

"The CB conversation."

"Who was with you?"

"My wife."

"What kind of car were you driving?"

"A 1977 Grand Prix."

"Did you have your CB radio on?"

"Yes."

"What channel were you monitoring?"

"Channel 19."

"How long did you converse with this youth as you proceeded southbound?"

"At least 15 minutes or more. It was at least a 10–mile stretch that I talked to him. We were probably traveling about 55 m.p.h. right after coming out of a bad stretch of fog. After we started talking we slowed down, way down, to maybe 40 to 45 miles per hour."

"Why?"

"Because I wanted to talk to that boy."

"Was your other radio on?"

"No, I had turned if off to hear better."

"Tell us what you heard."

"The boy was talking and no one was answering, but I answered."

"What was he saying that caused you to answer? Please be as descriptive as you can."

"I can't say exactly what he was saying before we hooked up on a two–way conversation. He was just trying to get someone to talk to him."

"Go on."

"He told me he had been to a party and that he had been drinking and that his friends had taken him out to a pick up truck so that he would not vomit on the floor because he was ill."

"Did you form any conclusions based upon the sound of his voice?"

"I assumed he was about 17, I don't know why."

"Did he tell you about himself?"

"Yes. He said that he used to live in Detroit and that his mother and father were divorced and that his mother had remarried and that they had moved to Whitfield."

"What else did you learn about him, from the CB conversation?"

"Just that he wasn't too pleased with his stepfather. I could relate to that because I had a stepfather so I tried to explain to him to give his new father a chance, you know."

"Were you able to form any opinion or conclusion as to his emotional state at that time?"

"Well he seemed depressed. He indicated that he was feeling bad."

"What was he depressed about?"

"Because his mother remarried and he had a stepfather and he felt the communication had broken down a little bit between he and his mother but he still felt they were very close and that he loved her very, very much and he kept repeating that."

"Did you talk to him about whether or not his mother knew where he was?"

"Yes. He said that his—I'm not sure—his friend or someone was supposed to have notified his mother as to his whereabouts. I then told him that his mother was probably worrying about him, and that, you know, he should go home, if that was possible."

"Was there any indication to you that the boy, even though he stated to you that he had been drinking, was drunk to the extent that his ability to speak was compromised, slurred speech, anything like that?"

"I never had to ask him to repeat or anything like that. I understood him perfectly."

"At that point was there any indication or not whether he was injured or had been in a fight, or any such thing?"

"No."

"Now was there a point in time when a third voice joined the conversation?"

"Yes."

"Please describe this voice and the conversation."

"A man's voice came on the CB. Almost from the beginning he wanted to know where the boy was located."

"Was there any doubt in your mind that the voice was a male?"

"No."

"Tell the court how this three way conversation went."

"It was not a three way conversation. The conversation was between the boy and myself. The other voice just kept asking the boy his location. I just assumed that this man was a man of authority of some sort because of the way he asked it. It was always 'son, where are you? What is your location?' It wasn't a polite voice like someone trying to help someone else out, it was constantly 'son, where are you, what is your location?' and he repeated that just before I lost contact with the boy."

"Did you form any impression as to what type of personality was demonstrated in this third voice?"

"Objection, objection, speculation, opinionated" yelled Pillister.

Judge Elkins: "Sustained. Please rephrase your question, Mr. Hatcher."

"What did he say to make you draw any conclusions?"

"It wasn't the words. It was the manner in which he asked the question. He spoke in a very firm voice as though he was interrogating the boy, and wanting to get to him."

"Did the boy ever respond to the inquiries of this male?"

"Not during the time I talked with him. Before I got home I intended to tell him not to answer this man."

"Why?"

"Because I didn't think the man meant him any good. I just felt that he—didn't mean the boy any good."

"Did you perceive in this voice that there was a threat?"

"I felt possibly this might be so, but, you know, he could have been even just a policeman that was trying to do his duty and arrest the boy before he got into trouble, but somehow I felt that he didn't mean the boy any good. I just felt that. I'd rather that the boy didn't answer him. I don't know what that man had in mind."

"Did you want the boy to give this voice his location?"

"Absolutely not. I was going to go back and try to locate him but I didn't. I'm sorry for that."

"Why didn't you want the boy to give this voice his location?"

"Because he was too persistent in wanting to know this boy's location."

"You were suspicious?"

"Yes, the voice never stopped. He just kept on trying to locate the boy."

"Based on the tone of the man's voice and the manner in which he inquired did you form any impression that you felt the boy would be comfortable giving this information out and did you have some perception of fear and danger?"

"Objection, your Honor. Once again the defense is trying to inject opinions into the mind of the witness. This witness does not know what this person is thinking, they are just his own feelings about what the other person was feeling."

Judge Elkins: "Objection sustained. The jury will please disregard the answer."

"That is all I have for this witness. Over to you Mr. Pillister."

Pillister got into his cross quickly, anxious to discredit the witness, distraught over this last minute twist that threatened to disrupt his whole efforts.

"Mr. Walkinshaw, you say it was only until you read this article in the paper about this case that you came forward?"

"Yes. I wasn't aware that anything was going on. I thought the thing was settled that the boy died of exposure and that was it.

No charges had been made or anything like that. I didn't want to come forward because I didn't see any point in upsetting the mother any further."

"You didn't see any point in coming forward with the possibility that there might be foul play?"

"No, because I felt that the police department, if there had been any indication of foul play would have found it. If there had been anything in the paper that indicated they ever suspected foul play I would have come forward. In fact, I had called the officer whose name appeared in the paper late one afternoon but he told me the case had all been settled."

Pillister started on his next question then abruptly cancelled it.

"Your Honor," he said, "the prosecution requests that this case be adjourned so that we can gather more facts on this sudden, upsetting development. We need more time. This witness was sprung on us without any prior warning."

Judge Elkins. "This is a bit unusual but since this testimony is 'out of the sky' so to speak, I have no objection to an adjournment, until 9:00 a.m. tomorrow morning."

When the doors to the courtroom opened the next day there was a long line of people waiting outside. All Detroit area media and all three–area television stations had picked up the sudden development in the case. It got top rating. "Mysterious CB Conversation Clouds Furman Trial" screamed the Herald. There was a scurrying for seats, so much so, that the sergeant at arms had to forcibly eject some who were too persistent.

Eye to eye, the assistant prosecuting attorney faced the witness. The trial was in the balance. If this were a cover up there could be no dilly–dallying. It would have to be squelched firmly and quickly.

"Mr. Walkinshaw, you testified yesterday that if you had read any possibility of foul play in the newspapers early in the case you would have come forward at a much earlier time to testify."

"Yes that is true."

"Now I would like to call your attention to this news article I am holding in my hand dated 20 days after the death of Tommy Furman. Would you please read the fifth line of this story and tell me whose name appears there."

"Your name, sir, the assistant prosecuting attorney, William Pillister."

"Now, sir you had some very important information about this case and the very first person you call is the defense attorney, didn't you?"

"The defense attorney was the first name I noticed in the case."

"Now you talked to some boy on a CB set on a certain date, what date was that sir?"

"I don't know. Whatever date they said it was. But I knew it was on a Saturday morning."

"In other words you don't really know the date that you talked to an unidentified boy but it's whatever date that Mr. Hatcher said it was."

"No, it was at the time of the party and everything because I was aware of it."

"Okay, Mr. Walkinshaw. I would like you to look at this news article from the *Oakland Herald* dated April 16, 1981 that appears in my hand and tell what you read in the headline."

"Two charged in Whitfield teen's death."

"And what about this one, a week later?"

"Probe into death of teenager continues."

"And this one, two months later."

"Tommy's Friends Describe His Life."

"And this one."

"Police: Liquor Factor in Youth's Death."

"And this one."

"Witness Stories Conflict."

"Okay, Mr. Walkinshaw do you and your wife subscribe to

the *Oakland Herald*?"

"Yes."

"And you mean to sit there and tell me in all honesty that you never read about this case in the paper until just recently just before you called Mr. Hatcher here?"

"I realize it seems that I wouldn't know but I honestly didn't. I would have come forward, honest. I called Mr. Hatcher because I have four children and I could see where Mr. Hunter might have bought some liquor or something and my children are grown up now so I've been through this whole pressure thing with children... 'Dad won't you?'"

"Okay, okay, let's go on. Now on the night in question, this boy didn't give you his name did he? Do you have any idea how many people have been remarried, having once lived in Detroit and brought their kids out to this area? He didn't say anything about Twin Oaks Farm, did he?"

"No."

"And there's another thing about this CB conversation. Did the truck Tommy was put in have any CB in it? We don't know that. And, have you ever experienced the phenomenon where maybe you're in the middle of traffic and you hear a guy behind you and this guy behind you is talking but the guy ahead of you never answers it because of the fact that this guy is out of range of the guy in back. And so the fact that this guy is out of range of the guy in back. And so you can hear both of them but they can't hear each other. Isn't it entirely possible that the menacing voice you heard was talking to someone else that you couldn't hear and not talking to the boy at all?"

"No, he was talking to the boy, in my opinion, because he kept asking him his location constantly."

"How do you know that he wasn't talking to a faint voice that was out of range and asking for that person's location? How many times did this person ask his location?"

"Several times. He continued to do so from the time I started talking to the boy until I lost the voice pattern."

"Your Honor, I am very suspicious about the testimony of this witness. Why did he not come to a law enforcement officer instead of the defense attorney when he had this information? How come he missed all of the articles in the paper when he subscribes to it? And his inability to identify the voice on the CB. I am suspicious but I will not dally this Court's time. Let us continue but I intend to bring this matter up again before this Court when I make my closing arguments."

Next to be called by the defense was Mrs. Walkinshaw. Like an obedient housewife she would duplicate her husband's story, perhaps adding a relish or two to show her feminine side.

"Mrs. Walkinshaw," said Hatcher, "did you substantially hear the same conversation on the CB radio as your husband has testified to in this court?"

"Yes. My husband wanted to relate to this boy that sometimes it takes time for a stepfather to show his love and to get to know his son, because my husband had a stepfather."

"Was the conversation perfectly clear to you on the CB, you don't have any hearing impairments and it was just as Mr. Walkinshaw said it was?"

"I have no hearing impairments and yes it was just like my husband said it happened."

"Will you please tell us why you didn't come forward with this information sooner than you did?"

"I felt like, well, what business was it of ours? If the boy wasn't driving, just sitting in the back seat of a pick up truck and then when we found out that they were accusing somebody of giving the boy alcohol then we decided to come forward."

"That is all I have for this witness."

"Mrs. Walkinshaw," Pillister began, "do you read the *Oakland Herald?*"

"Occasionally but usually not all the way through."

"And you don't remember reading in the newspaper any account of the death of Tommy Furman by alcohol and exposure?"

"No. As my husband said before he did make an attempt to contact a law enforcement officer about it but he said the case had already been closed so I thought what else could we do?"

"Mrs. Walkinshaw, what was your 'gut feeling' about your conversation with Tommy?"

It seemed that the prosecution was leading with that question. The chances were high that Mrs. Walkinshaw would repeat her husband's testimony about the rough voice on the CB. Or perhaps the prosecution was fishing and baiting the hook, seeking testimony that could be turned around to their advantage. But it was risky. Her answer could add kerosene to the fire of her husband's testimony.

"My 'gut feeling' was that the man either wanted to help him or harm him—my husband felt it was the latter."

The trap had been sprung. Pillister plunged ahead, opportunist that he was.

"Exactly, Mrs. Walkinshaw. What you just said is absolutely true. How do you know that the other person wasn't experiencing that exact same emotion, as you were experiencing and indeed wanted to help that young man instead of harming him? You don't know, do you?"

"No, I don't know. I don't know."

"That is all I have for this witness."

Pillister returned to his table satisfied that he had at least put a question mark on the Walkinshaw's testimony.

Hatcher, meanwhile, was springing his trap. It was another surprise twist.

"Your Honor, at this time I would like to withdraw my objection to Dr. Spiegle's testimony and move that his testimony that was stricken from the records regarding scratches on the back of Tommy's body occurred post mortem, after death, be allowed to stand."

Up and down. Up and down. For every hill to climb in this

case there was a downgrade around the next corner. Were there no straight–aways?

"If in fact," Hatcher said, "the scratches came after death left the body and these pictures were taken before the body was moved, the only logical conclusion would be that someone put the body in the field after death occurred and if that is the case and we have irrefutable testimony on these scratches, we don't have negligent homicide on the party of Mr. Conley, what we have here is some sort of homicide. And I would now make a motion to dismiss this case because, one, the people have not put forth a cogent case, and two, from an investigative standpoint there are many things lacking. And I think, perhaps, out there is a murderer floating around or someone, perhaps, who did this young boy in. That person took his pants down and sexually molested him. Why competent people were not involved in this investigation of all these other possibilities I'll never know but it's not right and it's not lawful to go and say that Robert Conley or James Hunter are criminally responsible for this case where so many intervening factors appear to have caused the death of Tommy Furman. I move to dismiss the case."

Pillister jumped to his feet, his voice came in quickly, staccato jerks.

"Your Honor, the prosecution has not completed its proofs yet. The defense has rested but the prosecution still has rebuttal witnesses. And I have an objection to the defense's unethical methods in which they ask that Dr. Spiegle's testimony about the scratches be put back into the record. They have already objected to the testimony and yet after they talk things over they decide it would be better for their cause if they left the testimony in. In other words they'll play their little game any way they want as long as they get their way. I find this trick very shabby and not a bit related to the case."

"Your objection is well taken, Mr. Pillister, and for the reasons you have given. The Court denies the dismissal. Continue Mr.

Pillister."

"Your Honor, the prosecution would like to call its final witness to the stand, Shelly Comstock."

Miss Comstock sort of danced her way to the witness chair. She wore fashion leggings in the style of the times. A teenager, her mouth chewed rapidly on a large stick of gum and her hands fidgeted nervously as the prosecutor prepared his questions.

Judge Elkins took one look at her and before even the first question was posed, wise to what happened before, said: "Miss Comstock please remove the gum from your mouth. It interferes with the court recorder getting your correct answers."

Quickly she removed the gum and then looked embarrassed as she sought some place to put it. He eyes strayed to the under part of the chair.

"Please Miss Comstock, not under the chair. Mr. Pillister would you please bring a piece of paper to the witness stand so Miss Comstock can have a place to deposit her gum."

Pillister, in his short career as a young prosecuting attorney had never come across a situation like this. He handled it skillfully with a touch of humor. He shuffled through a pile of papers, all with notes on them, then finally pulled out a blank sheet from his legal pad. All eyes turned towards him. Miss Comstock wadded up the gum in the paper and handed it back to him. Pillister made a quick movement like he was dribbling a basketball and launched a one handed jump shot. The paper hit the back of the wastebasket, ricocheted upwards and dropped neatly in for a two pointer. The crowed tittered.

Not to be outdone Judge Elkins countered "score a field goal for the Prosecution."

Hatcher stared stone–faced at the wall.

"And now that we've had our little comedy," said Judge Elkins, "let's go back to the reality of this courtroom and continue this case."

The crowd settled back, relaxed.

"Miss Comstock," said Pillister, "did you see either Mr. Conley or Mr. Hunter circulating around the Conley home while the party was in progress?"

"Yes, they would stop around and joke a little bit or ask how everything was going."

"So they knew, specifically, that drinking was going on at the party, right?"

"Yeah."

"Was Mr. Hunter or Mr. Conley present when Tommy was throwing up in the bathroom?"

"Yes, Mr. Hunter was. In fact he said someone should look into taking care of Tommy."

"But, he didn't offer to, did he?"

"Uh–uh."

"Was he present when Tommy was in the front seat of the pick up truck?"

"Uh–uh."

Judge Elkins looked suddenly over at the court recorder who by now was making frantic gestures towards the witness. She knew what all the distress was about. It was time for another lecture on teenage manners.

"Miss Comstock, would you please answer yes or no to the questions. The court recorder is having a hard time telling whether the uh–uh means yes or no. And please direct your voice to that door over there. I think you would be heard better instead of moving your face up and down. Now, Mr. Pillister please ask that last question again."

"Was Mr. Hunter present when Tommy was put in the back seat of the pick up truck?"

"I don't remember."

"The last time you saw Tommy, was his lip bruised or puffed?"

"Not that I seen, anyhow."

"Miss Comstock, had you been drinking at the party?"

"Yes."

"Were you 'drunk?'"

"Probably."

"Now, I would like to ask you a final question. Was there a CB unit in that truck?"

"Not that I know of."

"That is all for this witness."

Miss Comstock had been on the stand for less than five minutes. Her answers, however, brief as they were, were vital to the prosecution's case, especially about the CB unit.

"I would like to ask the witness what Tommy Furman was wearing the night of the party." It was Hatcher on cross.

"Tommy Furman was wearing a white insulated underwear shirt, jeans, blue tennis shoes and a denim vest."

"Not exactly suited for the weather at the time of the year was it?"

"No."

"So, if anyone were to blame for his demise it would have been Tommy himself who contributed to it."

Pillister was on his feet immediately.

"Objection: calls for a conclusion."

"Sustained. The jury will please disregard this last testimony."

"Was Tommy smoking any 'joints' when you saw him at the party, above and beyond the alcohol he had consumed?"

"Yes, he had been smoking on some joints that were passed around but they weren't his."

"And you saw him take three or four hits?"

"Well, there were seven or eight people around so he only got to hit it about twice because it only went around one time before it was gone."

"Did you have a chance to observe Tommy when he got to the party?"

"Yes."

"Did you see the bottle of Southern Comfort that he was carrying?"

"Yes."

"How full was it?"

"About half full."

"Was the bottle being passed around at the party?"

"Yes, there were three or four people that were slugging some of it down."

"The defense would like to emphasize to the Court at this time that not one but three or four people were passing around the bottle at some time during the party. In other words, Tommy was getting plenty of help in killing that bottle and he obviously couldn't have gotten drunk from the small amount that he consumed."

"Objection. Stating a fact not in evidence. Hearsay."

Judge Elkins: "I will take the answer to the question but ask the jury to disregard conclusion."

"Okay. Well, would you say that everyone was taking an equal amount out of the bottle?"

"No. There was one person who was hogging the bottle. I know he drank a lot of it because Tommy and his buddy got mad and they didn't want him to kill the whole bottle."

"How much joint smoking was going on?"

"Well, they had this guy out there demonstrating karate kicks, kicking at stuff, and stuff like that, and there was a group smoking on joints while all of this was going on."

"Did any of them take any marijuana into the house?"

"No. Mr. Hunter said he didn't want any pot smoking going on in his house."

"Who took Tommy out and laid him on the ground?"

"That was Mike Bettsler and Gerald Sommers."

"And who locked the door on him?"

"I did. He started to get up so I locked the door so he would not come in the house and get sick."

"Did anybody, and of the young people at the party, attempt to help Tommy in his condition?"

"Not exactly. I heard someone say 'don't let him have any more beer to drink' or something like that and someone suggested that we take him home, but no one did."

"In the manner that he was being taken outside did Tommy in any way resist this?"

"No."

"As far as you know was there any occasion that someone scratched part of Tommy's arm or inflicted any type of physical trauma on his body while he was being deposited outside?"

"No."

"That is all I have for this witness."

Judge Elkins: Mr. Pillister do you wish for redirect on this witness?"

"Yes your Honor, the prosecution has a few more questions."

"Miss Comstock," said Pillister, do you remember that about midnight Mr. Hunter went out and purchased an additional 12 pack of beer for the party?"

"Yes."

"Did Mr. Hunter bother to ask who was going to take care of Tommy and get him back home?"

"He asked who was going to take him home and I told him me and my boyfriend would see him home."

"But you didn't?"

"No."

"Did Mr. Hunter ever check back with you to see if you had followed through with your promise to see Tommy home?"

"No sir."

"Why didn't you take Tommy home as you promised?"

"I guess we got too involved with the party and besides he disappeared when we went to look for him."

"Your Honor that is all I have for this witness. The prosecution rests."

"Do you wish, Mr. Hatcher, for re–cross on this witness?"

"No, your Honor, the defense rests."

"Good," said Judge Elkins. "Before we get to summation arguments I note it is close to 5:00 p.m. so I will adjourn this case until tomorrow morning at 9:00 a.m. The sheriff will please remove the jury to their proper quarters. I again wish to caution the jury not to discuss this case among themselves, nor with anyone else. I warn them against listening to the radio, watching television or reading newspapers where this case is being discussed, so that they will not be prejudiced in making their decision."

The trial was winding down.

The jury returned with sharpened anticipation the next day. Usually the summation arguments are key blocks in the building or tearing down of a case as both the prosecution and the defense put in their final licks. If I knew Pillister his conclusions would be based on long research and faultless finding. On the other hand Hatcher was known to emotionally 'peak' a jury, playing all kinds of emotional tricks and maneuvers. It would be an interesting conclusion to a trial already known for suspenseful drama and electric moments.

Pillister led off.

"Your Honor, the prosecution would like to address the jury on the charges of Manslaughter, charges which we have proven beyond a shred of doubt are true and directed against the defendants. Now in Manslaughter, in Michigan, there are three choices. Involuntary Manslaughter is the mission to perform a legal duty. The courts have long recognized a duty on the behalf of adults not to furnish alcohol to a minor. The fact that Mr. Conley, by buying and furnishing a pint of Southern Comfort to the deceased, Thomas Furman, is guilty of this has been proven beyond a shadow of a doubt. Mr. Conley violated two statues of the law. The first was that alcoholic liquor should not be sold or furnished to a person unless that person has reached the age of 21 years. A person who does so is guilty of a misdemeanor under Michigan law. Also, Mr. Conley violated that statute commonly known as contributing to the delinquency of a minor. Any person who causes a child under the age of 17 to become delinquent so as to come under the jurisdiction of the juvenile court is guilty of this offense."

"Another element of the case," said Pillister, "is that the defendant knew of the facts giving rise to a duty of caring for the victim and another element is that the defendant willfully neglected the duty and was grossly negligent in doing so. Gross negligence is defined as that the defendant knew of a danger and ordinary care was required to avoid injury of another and that the defendant had the ability to avoid harm by the exercise of ordinary care but failed to use such ordinary care when it must have been apparent that the result was likely to cause harm; and the death of Thomas Furman was directly caused by the defendant."

"Conley," Pillister said, "was directly responsible for failing to perform the duties set forth by the statutes. So, Tommy is saying that he wants Southern Comfort and Conley is suggesting that he shouldn't drink hard liquor. On page 324 of the transcript we have Mike Dooley testifying 'Yeah, he (Mr. Conley) suggested that we shouldn't drink it really.' This is crucial because when you're talking gross negligence you're talking about somebody who foresees something of the type of thing that happened, or in this case, might happen. We don't have to guess. He, Mr. Conley stated it directly to a witness."

"And why shouldn't a young person like that, an inexperienced drinker, pick up a bottle of Southern Comfort," Pillister argued. "Why shouldn't he 'hit' on hard liquor? Why, Judge Elkins, because the common phrase is 'likker is quikker.' Even his buddy said this. He kept passing it back and forth to Tommy. Southern Comfort is a nice sweet liquor and you can pass it down and drink and it tastes good. Only, to a young 15–year–old it's like handing him a loaded shotgun. And because it tastes so sweet and nice a young person will 'slam it down.' And they will get drunk fast. And that's exactly what happened here. Gross Negligence. We're not talking 16, 18 or 20 years of age; we're talking a full six years under the drinking age. This further emphasizes the reckless and wanton conduct of Mr. Conley and brings actions well above ordinary negligence to gross negligence. Act 16403 is commonly known as misdemeanor manslaughter. 16404 is the theory set forth wherein the defendant commits gross negligence. Act 16404 is the obligation to perform a legal duty. The next theory is the Misdemeanor Manslaughter embodied and the elements present when Tommy Furman died. The element that the death was caused by an act of the defendant. He was committing an unlawful act, which was inherently and naturally dangerous to human life, that which was grossly negligent to human life. Inherently and naturally dangerous does not mean that death or injury is imminent or that it's likely or that it is probable but rather when you think that it is inherently and naturally hazardous; that is, things that might happen."

"In the People versus Ogg, 26 Mich. App 372, 1970 involving contributing to the delinquency of a minor and coupled with negligence occurred when there was a fire and the children were burned to death, and where the parents were supposed to be looking after their children and weren't. Another case occurred where someone admitted an overdose of Heroin and manslaughter charges were sustained on an appeal. The People have fulfilled our burden of proof on Mr. Conley. He provided Tommy with alcohol. He knew he shouldn't have done it. It was clearly a case of gross negligence dealing with causation later."

"And now we turn to Mr. Hunter, who was the gracious hospitable host for this illegal teenage party. By allowing minors to possess and consume alcohol on his premises he is violating the act dealing with contributing to the delinquency of a minor. The minors, in this case, were violating the statute that makes it an offense to possess alcohol. And the second element of the law deals with the affirmative duty of Mr. Hunter to care for Mr. Furman. At the point when he encountered Mr. Furman on the floor of his house and near the bathroom and he saw him in a comatose or semi–comatose state he should have done something about it. The jury should be aware that in the state of Michigan there is a statute called the 'rescue doctrine' and that there is an affirmative duty to rescue a person who is in dire distress. I would like to point to the case of Farwell versus Keaton where two young men went out and engaged in a little horse play and they got thrashed by somebody else. One of the parties was injured and his buddy put him in the back seat and drove around. And his buddy didn't offer to take him to a hospital yet he knew he was seriously injured. He didn't take him to his relatives he didn't do anything. He just let him be and dropped him off at his folk's house, not even ringing the doorbell."

"The ensuing lawsuit upheld the rescue doctrine and the duty to properly care for someone in distress."

"In the same way it was Mr. Hunter's duty, seeing young Tommy in a comatose or semi–comatose state on the floor, to call his parents. But he didn't call his parents. He did not call medical authorities even though he had somebody who was passed out drunk and we all know people sometimes die from alcohol overdose. In the Farwell versus Keaton case a young man and his companion were partners in a social venture and that social venture ended in injury to one. It is implicit that in such a common undertaking there is a duty to render assistance to the other when he is in peril, if he can do so without endangering himself. Whether Tommy was comatose on the floor because of the alcohol that Mr. Hunter had allowed him to consume in his house along with the other minors, or whether he was knocked out because of a blow to the mouth, as Mr. Hatcher has here suggested, somebody had an affirmative duty to help him in his plight. And Mr. Hunter, the older adult at the party, and knowing of the peril of the situation, should have been that somebody."

# The Party at Twin Oaks Ranch

"In the case of Dupuis versus Flateu, Michigan Supreme Court, a guest became intoxicated and the guest went outside to try and get home. The guest said he was too drunk and wanted to stay at the home. The host put him on a horse and wagon; that person fell off the horse and wagon and nearly froze to death, suffering grievous injury. Now that is the affirmative duty we are talking about and that which the Michigan Supreme Court has ruled on, whether civil or criminal. Manslaughter is the only crime on the books where there is not a culpable state of mind defined. All there is, is negligence with something else, making it either gross negligence or misdemeanor in a manslaughter or whatever, so it is completely relevant to this case."

"The next principle set forth in Manslaughter, as in the Far-well versus Keaton case, further outlines the principles of the rescue doctrine. It is simply stated as: 'if you engage upon a cause of action to assist somebody—and this is a law school law—you have to follow it through."

Judge Elkins: "It's the Good Samaritan Doctrine."

"That's correct. And I now refer you to pages 375–380 in the transcript. Mr. Hunter is now in the presence of Mr. Furman who is on the bathroom floor. Mr. Hunter asks 'who is going to take him home?' And whom did he ask? He just asked generally 'who's going to take the kid home?' Shelly Comstock testified, 'I will, me and my boyfriend will take him home.' And where was her boyfriend? Was he in the immediate vicinity? No, he was in the back room. Shelly didn't know at the time whether her boyfriend would or would not condescend to take Tommy home. Okay, let's go on. Mr. Hunter is the only parental figure on the scene. He says 'who's going to take this kid home?' and Shelly says that she and her boy friend will. Her boyfriend isn't around and Shelly is a girl who's just turned 17. She testified on page 370, that she herself was drunk. She states that she herself does not have transportation available but that she is relying on someone else. On page 378 of the transcript it shows that Hunter never bothered to follow up and see if she and her boyfriend took Tommy home. He never checked to see if this intoxicated 17 year old girl or her boyfriend in another room took Tommy home. Now is that recklessness? Is that gross negligence? The People charge that that is exactly what the statute is talking about."

"Mr. Hunter created the peril here by allowing these young, minor children to have the party that they did, in his home. Our only burden at this trial is that we establish a prima facia case of causation. Some scintilla of evidence has come in that there might be another cause. We have brought out the Hypothermia philosophy where it is a fact that in hypothermia there is an inherent tendency to take off one's clothes. You remember the testimony that the shoes were laid nice and neat over by the fence right next to each other and that his pants were drawn down around his knees. I suggest that we are NOT dealing with mere suspicion here. All of the stated evidence before the court supports Tommy walked over to that field himself, took off his shoes over by the fence and continued walking in a line towards his house, trying to get home and that he was hypothermiated while he was out there. He was only wearing a pair of blue jeans, tennis shoes, long sleeved underwear and denim vest. That was it. Nothing else. He got drunk and he hypothermiated there. And God knows how many hours he floundered around out there in the field, falling down and hitting his face, causing small scratches on his body and I suggest even putting those scratches on his buttocks, but I think Dr. Spiegle was wholly wrong that it was post mortem injury. And about what happened to Dr. Spiegle's testimony in this case. We find the defense is willing to challenge Dr. Spiegle on 99 points out of 100. They say Dr. Spiegle is wholly incompetent to testify but the one thing that Dr. Spiegle says that will benefit their case they back him up 100 percent."

Pillister turned to drink a quick glass of water, striding slowly to his table. Then he abruptly pivoted and quickly returned to the jury box where 12 sets of eyes bore down on him, listening to every word.

"Now I am almost certain that our learned opponent on the defense is going to shoot at this jury 'why hasn't the Prosecution charged every person who was over the legal age of majority with this crime?' Quite simply, ladies and gentlemen, not everybody there was a host as is endorsed by the Michigan law, imposing a duty. Not everybody there created the peril, as did Mr. Hunter by having the party at his house. So let's put a rest to this little plot right now."

"I suggest to this Court that every case you have seen in a Circuit Court trial has some misleading issues that can confuse a jury but we don't come in here trying to present any issues beyond a reasonable doubt and that's what the law says we have to do. Next I would direct your attention to the case involving the People versus Shirley Finney where children were in a locked house with matches. It was a reasonable, foreseeable act that those kids would get those matches and burn the house down and die from a causal connection. This all comes under the heading of adult negligence."

"And now we come to the mysterious, last minute Citizens Band conversation between two people driving down I-75 in the middle of the night. They pick up a mysterious CB conversation Tommy Furman had with anybody. We asked Mr. Walkinshaw the date of the conversation and he replied that it was whatever date the defense said it was. How many couples from Detroit, divorced, and remarried, come to this part of the state? A great many I would say. And we have the word of Detective Hansard that there was more than one teenage party going on right in that area that night. So how can the CB incident be tracked to the Hunter home and Tommy Furman? We say there may be some coincidences in that CB conversation but there is no flat–out voice identification, nor can the defense prove that that conversation emanated from the back of the pick up truck where Tommy was allegedly placed. It could have come from any of those parties."

Pillister was going at a furious pace now. His sentences were brief, hitting painfully home in short thrusts, keeping pace with the quick–as–lightening probes of an alert mind.

"The amazing thing is that although both Mr. and Mrs. Walkinshaw are subscribers to the *Oakland Herald* they waited for two years to contact someone about this case just before it came to trial even though there were big black headlines on the case nearly every day for three weeks. And then, when they finally do read about it, they say, for some strange reason or other they go to the defense attorney. Anyone else with this information would take it to a law enforcement officer. They sat on it for 2 1/2 years before revealing it. I find that utterly amazing."

"And now Mr. Hatcher wants the Court to believe that there's foul play here, that Tommy's body was put there after-wards. If so, how did he die? Did he die right behind the door after allegedly being put out there by two teenagers? Did he die of exposure somewhere else and someone moved him to his final resting–place? If that is true, where is the evidence of murder? The strangulation marks, the needle holes the stab wounds or what? Mr. Hatcher has raised speculation that is totally lacking in evidence. Everybody that saw Tommy that night said they saw him falling down drunk. All of the evidence suggests exposure and many circumstances suggest he walked out there under his own violation."

"Then, we have the defense glibly shifting gears, calling Dr. Spiegle's testimony alternately competent and incompetent, depending on whether it will help their case. I remind you another court has already ruled on the expertise, the training of Dr. Spiegle and has concluded that he was legally competent to testify. Regardless of what civil action is going against him, which up to now has not been proven, you have to accept that testimony as expert testimony. Notwithstanding your personal opinions of Dr. Spiegle and shouting, sensational headlines in the newspaper about his work remember, he has been reinstated by the Medical Board and allowed to practice medicine pending the court trial. And according to the law of our land, thank God, a person is presumed innocent until proven guilty beyond a shadow of a doubt."

The defense has pulled all kinds of tricks in this case, even suggesting in your minds that 'there is a murderer running loose out there.' They suggest in melodramatic fashion that 'someone done Tommy in.' And I suggest to you, ladies and gentlemen, that there is NO murderer out there. If anyone is to blame for the death of Tommy Furman in that field it is Mr. Conley and Mr. Hunter who by their adult·negligence and irresponsibility allowed Tommy to go beyond his ability to control his young mind and allowed him to perish by exposure. They are to blame for Tommy's demise, not an 'unknown murderer out there.' This is nothing more than a smoke screen in the mind of Mr. Hatcher to confuse the issue."

"I have nothing more to say ladies and gentlemen. It has been a long, drawn out trial with many unexplained issues and I think that this jury in good conscience cannot render any other decision than to find the defendants guilty as charged."

Wiping perspiration from his brow, Pillister strode slowly to his seat. He looked beat. His emotional appeal to the jury had drained him. The prosecution had done its job beautifully. In rapid–fire sequence they had built a masterful case, block by block, like a master builder constructing a house.

Hatcher walked quickly to the jury box. His job admittedly would be difficult. Not only would he have to tear down the prosecutor's case but also he would have to be careful doing it. Pillister had already made quite an impression of honesty and resourcefulness before the jury. His research admittedly had been faultless, his delivery straightforward and earnest.

"I would like to compliment the vigorous, young prosecuting attorney on his presentation," Hatcher began. He wanted the jury to know that he held no grudges, no anger towards his aggressive opponent. That would mean getting off on the wrong foot right off the bat."

"His summation to the jury was magnificent and dedicated. No, I will say to you I find no fault with the execution, only the logic. But, ladies and gentlemen, this is not a dramatic play that is going on here it is a law case. The fate of two men, in the manhood of their life, is at stake. They could face imprisonment for a crime for which there was no passion, only sadness and grief. If they could have their way Tommy would be alive today and playing tennis on the Whitfield tennis team, dating a young girl, going to a dance, perhaps, or watching the Tigers play baseball on TV. Unfortunately, however, Tommy is dead. And his death is not a crime against Mr. Hunter or Mr. Conley. It is a crime against society. It is a crime against the morals of that society."

"For how many of you have come up against the age old generation gap, the pitting of father against son, mother against daughter. How many of you have heard your daughter or son say, 'Hey dad, don't be an old stick in the mud, let us have some fun.' You were young yourself. The expression is age old. The implications are also very old. If you do you're in with the gang, a part of the group, respected, honored, and looked up to. If you don't you're an old stick in the mud, someone out of the dark ages. I wonder what you would have done in this case? How many of you have had graduation parties in your home? Are there any of you, who have not allowed the kids to have a beer or two as long as they kept things down? But many times one or two have gotten a little out of line. Of course you tried to keep things cool but isn't it a pretty big job to keep a line on 15 or 20 kids, especially if they're teenagers? Can any of you absolutely say for certain that you have never faced this situation? And can any of you say that for the grace of God you might be in the same position that Mr. Hunter and Mr. Conley are facing right now in this courtroom?"

"Yes, there were many intervening factors going on at that party that night. There were also people coming and going. There were other adults there, too, besides Mr. Conley and Mr. Hunter. Who is to say where the responsibility belongs? Why Mr. Conley and Mr. Hunter? They were older, yes, but age is not necessarily a criteria of maturity. A lot of those young adults could have and should have taken a hand in the situation."

Hatcher looked around the jury box to see if his words were making their mark. They were. Some had their mouths open, hanging on every word. Others tensed forward, looking him directly in the eyes. It was almost a duplicate of the Prosecution's effort. This jury seemed dedicated, determined to reach a fair verdict in spite of the emotional issues involved.

"Now I've researched the law quite thoroughly and the transcript of this case, and I will tell you right now that Mr. Pillister has set a new record in stretching the truth. What he said witnesses were saying was not coming from that stand. He neatly tucked into a corner, only mentioning, that one of the witnesses, Mike Dooley, testified that Tommy, when last seen did not have any bruises on his lips or a puffed eye. That all happened later. And we still say someone who had murder in their heart against Tommy could have done it. Now in a charge of Manslaughter you must show that a duty exists to take care of someone in danger and you must show that by breaching that duty the act was the—and I emphasize this—proximate cause of death. I don't recall that the prosecution has firmly established a proximate cause of death. Even the Prosecution's expert witness, Dr. Spiegle, the one they would have you believe is capable of expert testimony, admitted in his report the cause of death was only 'probable.'"

"The use of alcohol in our society today is very, very common. Young boys experiment with alcohol. Young boys drink alcohol and young boys pass out from drinking alcohol. Where Mr. Pillister tells you its the same as handing a boy a loaded shot gun or giving a young toddler matches to play with, he's all wet. It's not the same thing as seeing a man fall off a boat and rescuing him. Young boys pass out, then lie there and they wake up, and they're okay. Mr. Pillister would have you believing that any adult has a duty to a minor for their safety. Now I submit to you that there was more than one adult at this party. Is Mr. Hunter charged because he was simply the oldest adult person there? Then I say that's weird thinking."

"We have heard testimony that Mr. Furman was staggering. I don't see any testimony that he had completely passed out. In testimony it was pointed out that Mr. Hunter was inquiring about whom was going to take that person home. One girl said 'we will.' Well, why isn't that person here in court being charged in this case? Why aren't the ones who lugged him out to the pick up truck charged for breaching their duty? And how about the young girl who locked the door so Tommy wouldn't come into the house and vomit? Isn't she to blame, also for Tommy's death?"

"And we have Mr. Pillister's own expert witness, and I will be the first to admit that he is suspect, say that the scratches on Tommy's body were caused by attendants moving him to the ambulance. Now I tell you those scratches were an inch to an inch and a half in length. I ask you how come expert ambulance attendants; skilled and trained in their jobs with years of experience and adept in the handling of injured or deceased persons could cause scratches on young Tommy's body. No, they did not inflict those scratches. The only thing we can assume is that whoever put Tommy out there, somebody who wanted to do him in, inflicted those scratches."

Hatcher paused to let this sink in. He adroitly back peddled, all the time writing notes on his legal pad, while the jury pondered his words. It was a ploy to emphasize his point and allow the jury more time to deliberate. Fully a minute elapsed before he broke the silence.

"Involuntary Manslaughter is the killing of another without malice and unintentionally by paraphrasing a negligent omission to perform a duty or by some other intentional means. The issue in respect to Mr. Conley and Mr. Hunter is did they kill Tommy Furman? I would be the first to admit that since there is no other anatomical evidence as to cause of death that it is reasonable to assume that based on the testimony of pathologists that the cause of death was exposure to the elements. But, I say, so what? In order to establish that Robert S. Conley and James W. Hunter killed Thomas Furman by exposure, there is this missing link. The Prosecution must bring out clear cut, beyond doubt, evidence how Thomas Furman got there to be exposed. And that is the big, complex problem. Because there's absolutely no way that one can conclude that Thomas Furman died by exposure due to Mr. Robert S. Conley and or Mr. James W. Hunter. And the prosecution has not proved that."

"There was marijuana, there was perhaps Mescaline at that party. Neither Mr. Hunter nor Mr. Conley brought those drugs to that party. It was obviously supplied but not by Mr. Hunter or Mr. Conley. And that is the point. Had they only left Tommy in the bathroom to sleep off his intoxication, whatever the degree was, he would have never died of exposure. Now that is an intervening cause. So how can anyone say that Mr. Hunter or Mr. Conley killed Tommy Furman? The more likely cause are the two boys who carried him out because certainly had this not been done he would have remained there and never would have been exposed to the elements."

"Secondly, we have even suspicion of foul play regardless of Mr. Pillister's remarks on this. All Mr. Pillister did was indicate that there was some sort of documentation somewhere in the journals of Medical Science of a case of hypothermia, not necessarily involving the ingestion of alcohol, but he doesn't know. And I wonder why the prosecution wasn't interested in refuting the obvious intervening cause problem? And neither did any of the Prosecution witnesses address that problem. Maybe he didn't want to give it further credence. But, be that as it may, it's quite possible that someone didn't want a dead body lying next to the house. It's entirely possible. Maybe Tommy was sexually assaulted. We'll never know because nobody bothered to check on that in spite of evidence supporting that theory, like blue jeans pulled down over the buttocks, a fat lip and long scratches on the body. And they failed to examine the seminal vesicles for evidence of sexual foul play. I'll still stick by my statement that a proper investigation was not made on this case and that foul play is a definite possibility."

"And regardless of what Mr. Pillister would have you believe about Mr. and Mrs. Walkinshaw I think that they were courageous in coming here to testify. I ask you ladies and gentlemen of the jury, how many of you read a newspaper from cover to cover? Most of us don't read every last detail on each page; we read by glancing at stories. I think their testimony that Tommy could talk coherently and their belief that he was not dead drunk is important. And about the missing CB unit from the pick up truck. Did anybody ever consider that there are portable CB units that can be removed to another location and not permanently attached to a car or truck?"

"We have had a lot of theories expressed by the prosecution as to how Tommy met his demise but there has been no hard evidence. And that, ladies and gentlemen is what you're sitting in that jury box for. Remember the law is presumed innocence until proven guilty beyond a shadow of a doubt. One of the prosecution's theories is a cock and bull story about hypothermia. Remember they said it was related to stories from the Germans about prisoners in World War II camps. Yet when I asked them they didn't know the research book the studies were made from nor could they substantiate anything about the theory except someone remembered reading about it somewhere. The study, if it existed, probably made interesting reading before some egghead professor seeking a degree for his thesis. It may or may not be true so remember you are dealing with 'beyond reasonable doubt' not someone's thesis."

"Again we want to point out the discrepancy in the prosecution's case concerning giving Tommy that 100 proof Southern Comfort. We don't dispute that 'likker is quikker' but there were several young men dragging on that bottle. And one young man was hogging the bottle so much that Tommy and his friend got mad at him. How much of that Southern Comfort did Tommy drain off and how much others drank is unknown and nothing has been offered as hard evidence about how much was consumed by other parties and how much went down Tommy's throat. Finally there has been a lot of testimony on how drunk Tommy was or could have been. We have heard testimony that that could depend upon the condition of his liver, whether he had any greasy food in his stomach, his ability to pass off alcohol by metabolism, whether he vomited and the percentage of alcohol in the beer he consumed. I suggest to this jury that absent a breathalyzer test at the time he was alive there is no way possible for anyone to determine whether Tommy was drunk, moderately drunk or cold sober when he wondered away from that party. But one thing is certain. At the time the boy was talking to Mr. and Mrs. Walkinshaw he was coherent. And what about the puffed upper and lower lip? Did someone slug him and then he started staggering because of the concussive effect? Even the Prosecution's witness admits that this could have occurred, that he fell down and stayed in the field. That's certainly an intervening cause. That's very possible even if you don't pay any attention to the logical and highly likely suggestion that the boy was a victim of foul play."

"There was no witness that saw Tommy wandering around in that field that night. So what do we have? Mostly theories about what happened. But I tell you now that a logical theory, besides the foul play possibility, is that somebody at that party decked him right smack in the lip. And that blow had a concussive effect on Tommy and he just said to himself 'well I've had enough of this and I'm going home.' So, the combination of the blow to the head, plus his ingestion of alcohol, whatever that amount was, and that still hasn't been proven, is also a strong point in the favor of that theory, that he passed out in the field. So it wasn't all the alcohol that caused Tommy's death, some of it was physical injury. And that injury, I emphasize, was not caused by either Mr. Conley or

Mr. Hunter. So again we have the examples of intervening causes. In the People versus Scott it says that the prosecution, to come forth with a conviction for Involuntary Manslaughter, must prove that the conduct of the defendants in allegedly killing the deceased was the proximate cause. In the light of the controlling law and the moor of facts concerning what happened before, the jury has no choice but to dismiss this case and set these innocent people free and if the law wants to reinvestigate and make a determination of who did what to Tommy Furman and who done him in, if that is the case maybe they would have an argument. I strongly believe that this was not manslaughter. There are substantial facts which allow one to strongly suspect that there was a homicide in this case, an intentional killing and had nothing to do with the defendants, Mr. Conley and Mr. Hunter."

"And lastly, let us go back to some of the background facts surrounding the party at Twin Oaks. There were 25 to 30 people milling around at the party, some of them young adults. They were coming and going. Who knows what they were bringing into that party? Were there any of those young people checking each other as they came in, and who would do that anyhow? So this is a lot different from the case where the children were locked into a home and left to carelessly play with matches. It is quite clear to sustain a conviction for manslaughter the conduct of the accused must be and have been the eminent and direct cause of death. So, if the garage repairman repairs your brakes incorrectly and you run into the back of someone else's car and hurt somebody, then the garage man is at fault. But no one would be at fault if a pedestrian died of a heart attack on the side of the road and someone hit him because he was lying in the road. There is an obvious problem there of proving negligence."

"Personally it is a great tragedy that this young man had to die. He was a fine looking young man perhaps ready to turn around his up and down life at this point. His parents should have our condolences because they have suffered a grievous loss that can never be replaced. And if young Tommy Furman had been the only guest at the party there would perhaps be justification for charging Mr. Conley and Mr. Hunter with this crime. But there you have many factors and many different situations. And who knows or can recall what actually went on? Some of the guests were admittedly under the influence of alcohol brought in by their adult peers, not primarily by Mr. Hunter or Mr. Conley. And certainly it was not the natural or necessary result of the acts of the defendants. Many of you are aware that this is a landmark case as the Prosecution has so ably pointed out. Once in the law case file it will be used again and again to sustain involuntary manslaughter charges against unwitting hosts who open their homes so that young people can gather and have fun. And isn't it better to have a home atmosphere at such parties rather than to have them out in a field, a 'Grasser Party' where there is no control at all and where booze and drugs run rampant? Remember, if you take these parties out of the home they go underground. They take to the fields; they misrepresent their age at taverns; they go to vacant barns and buildings where they can engage in immoral acts, in addition to drinking booze."

"So, if you sustain a conviction of manslaughter here you are literally condemning hundreds or perhaps thousands of others to the same fate as Mr. Hunter and Mr. Conley. And remember one of you in this courtroom today could someday be put in the same situation as the defendants. I repeat there is only one choice in this case, the right choice, and that is to dismiss the charges against these defendants and let these innocent men go free. The defense rests, your Honor."

It was over. The arguments, the rebuttals, the direct and redirect examinations, the cross and recross, the drama, the excitement, the surprises, the debates.

The big element was to come, the jury's decision. The prosecution and defense both agreed it was a "landmark case." They (the defense) would have you believe that if the charges were upheld every parental host who held a graduation party, a birthday party, or any other social gathering where there was drinking and teenagers would now be suspect for Involuntary Manslaughter, that such parties, if allowed to take place outside the house, would degenerate into field maneuvers of sex and alcoholic orgies, all without controls. But, checking out the other side, adults would not be mandated to exert responsibility at such parties, monitor all party areas, check constantly to see that nothing improper was taking place; that booze and drugs were held to a minimum and those who got into a situation where they were behaving insensibly would be promptly taken home by responsible adults. It was a decision not to be taken lightly. Sociological mores and old hardbound traditions were at the crossroads. Which was right?

I sat there thinking of all of this, wondering how to write it all into a sensible, interesting news story. It would be hard to keep Mike Dunn out of it that was for sure. Again, the perennial dilemma I had faced time and time again.

My thoughts jolted suddenly into reality.

Judge Elkins was speaking. She was talking slow and deliberate, emphasizing each word as she gave instructions to the jury about their duties regarding the laws of Manslaughter, their responsibilities on presumed innocence until proven guilty and finally to keep bias out of their verdict and not be influenced by the words and actions of others.

"Swear in an officer, please, clerk," she said.

The clerk strode forward, administered the oath to a fellow officer of the court, James Whittier.

"You do solemnly swear that you will, to the utmost of your ability, keep the persons sworn as jurors in this trial in some private convenient place; that you will suffer no communication, orally or otherwise, to be made to them; that you will not communicate with them yourself, orally or otherwise, unless ordered by the Court; and that you will not, until they shall have rendered their verdict, communicate to anyone the state of their deliberations or the verdict that they may have agreed upon, so help you God."

"I do," said Whittier. He then beckoned to the jurors and led them to the jury room.

"You have orders from the Court to arrange for a warm meal to be brought in to them," said Judge Elkins.

Slowly the courtroom cleared. Both attorneys gathered up their papers and prepared to depart. They would probably go out for dinner, leaving instructions with lesser members of their firm to promptly notify them when the jury returned.

I watched Mrs. Furman. She was still sitting in the front row. Her eyes had never left the defendants, darting from one to the other, with an occasional look at the Judge or the attorneys whenever an important point was made.

Both defendants reacted to the steady stare by shifting uneasily in their chairs; their eyes purposely shifted away from the solitary, sad figure, Mrs. Furman.

Mr. Furman, seated beside his wife, put his arm around her shoulder and led her away. She seemed stopped by her burden, a sorrowful little woman enmeshed in the biggest tragedy of her life. They were the last ones out of the courtroom except myself. I was still looking over my notes.

"You must leave now, we are clearing the courtroom," said the bailiff.

I thanked him and walked out the door to a nearby restaurant, "The Green Parrot." I made a call to Kris and a couple of other calls to the newspaper office telling them that the jury was out. I picked away at the food absently. It was the "Happy Hour" and the crowd was in a jovial mood, everybody talking and laughing. But I wasn't happy. My favorite drink, a Martini, had failed to lessen the foreboding I had about this case. I knew how I felt. I wouldn't write it that way, of course, but I wanted a conviction in the worst way. I had seen teenage parties like this get out of hand. I had seen my teenage brother passed out in our living room after a wee hours graduation party where his buddy drove onto the wrong driveway and got stuck in a culvert. Sleepily, as a young teenager, I walked out to noises in the living room where my mom and dad were watching television over the prostrate form of a young man on the rug, my brother. He had a towel under his mouth to catch the vomit. By the luck of God he had staggered safely home. His buddy, who lived down the block a couple of houses, made it home before collapsing in a drunken stupor on the doorstep after he had rung the door bell. His parents picked him up and brought him in.

"How many times has this scene been repeated," I thought. "Too many."

I thought of the many fatal accidents I had reported, many caused by young alcoholic minds confused by too much beer, behind the wheel of a car out of control crashing into an immovable object, a tree. The sight wasn't beautiful. In many cases the victim survived only to live a life of paralysis, numb beyond the waist upward. True, some of the victims were dead not because of inadequate adult supervision but as a result of their own senseless overindulgence, and insistence of other teenagers that they "have one more drink for the road." But there were many others where responsible parents could have prevented tragedy.

Both attorneys had presented their cases well but I had misgivings about the verdict, feeling that peer pressure would prevail instead of common sense.

I was through with the salad and most of the way through the main entree when I felt a gentle thrust on my shoulder. It was now about two hours after the jury had left for deliberations.

"They're coming back now, I thought you would like to know," it was the Bailiff talking. A subscriber and strong supporter of The Herald he had seen me leave for the restaurant.

"Thanks" I said. I bolted down the remaining portions of my meal, hurriedly put on my coat and walked quickly to the courtroom.

The Judge, in splendorous black robe, was back at her seat. The jury had filed in and taken their seats.

Judge Elkins held up her hand. The courtroom was hushed. "Before any verdict is reached I would like to say that I will stand for no demonstrations, no shouting or ravings that would upset the dignity of this Court. If there is such a disturbance, I will stop the proceedings immediately and clear the courtroom. Proceed with the questioning of the jury, Mr. Clerk."

The clerk rose and turned towards the jury. The courtroom was strangely, eerily quiet except for the nervous stirring of feet.

"Members of the jury have you agreed upon a verdict, and if so, who will speak for you?"

"We have." It was the jury foreman speaking. "I am the foreman and I will speak for my fellow jurors."

"What is your verdict?"

"We dismiss this case and find the defendants not guilty by reason of causation—the defendants were not the imminent and direct cause of death of the deceased. We also find several intervening factors not directly attributable to the defendants."

The clerk quickly pressed on, aware that the most important part was now over, but nevertheless realizing that routine measures still remained. The judge held up her hand again to quiet the crowd as the final official act was put in motion.

"Please," she said, "this case is not ended. Will the clerk please continue with the instructions to the jury."

"Members of the jury," said the clerk, "listen to your verdict as recorded. You do say upon your oaths that you dismiss this case by reason of causation. So say you, Mr. Foreman. So say you all members of the jury?"

All 12 voices answered in the affirmative but their vocal efforts were lost in a bedlam of sobbing, crying, shouting, screaming that crescendos like a spouting volcano. Judge Elkins held up her gavel threateningly but relented and decided to let the crowd have its way.

The two defendants went quickly to their attorney where a full minute of hand shaking and violent bear hugs ensued. Mrs. Furman looked passively at the scene and tears were visible as she was led shaking out of the courtroom by her compassionate husband. I didn't have the heart to interview her. Perhaps later.

Judge Elkins grabbed her notes and was preparing to leave. She gathered up her robe and turned but I intercepted her before she made it to the doorway.

"Judge Elkins," I said, "may I have a few words with you before your leave?"

"Yes certainly. You are—?"

"Mike Dunn of the *Oakland Herald*."

"What is it you want?"

"I would like to ask you some of your feelings about the case."

"I'm afraid I can't discuss all of them. This case may go to appeal, you know, but I can give you a couple of candid thoughts, within the realm of jurisdiction."

"Okay."

"First of all I thought the case was well tried. I intend to commend both attorneys on their resourcefulness. I think it was a great tragedy that this young man died, so young in life. But truthfully it was outside the limits of the Good Samaritan doctrine and there were a host of intervening causes that could have led to that young man's death. I 'm not sure what will happen now. There could still be civil damages, but that is not my department. And it's not necessarily back to square one; there is a complete review of this case available to both attorneys in case of appellate review. Because of the complexity of situations and theories I do find an obvious problem with proximate cause and the jury agreed. And that, young man, is all that I will say."

"Thank you."

The courtroom emptied but I heard eerie echoes of voices debating blood/alcohol readings, the pleadings of a young man in trouble heard over a CB radio, the high pitched voice of a 14 year old girl describing how she had been addicted to alcohol since she was 12. The case was in my system, too much so. I had to do something to get me out of it.

It was now 4:30 p.m. Too late to start on the story. Besides I had a few loose ends that were still dangling. I had heard from Deputy Sheriff Hansard that he had asked the Walkinshaws to take a lie detector test and that they had refused on the advice of Hatcher. And now that he had won the case it would be asinine for Hatcher to blow it on the whims of a machine, particularly if an appeal came up where the test could be a psychological factors. Although not admissible in court it was a powerful weapon against the defense if the results were positive that they were lying. There are always devious means to get the test into the record without getting an outright yes or no answer. It would be worthwhile to check it out. Hansard told me: "They (the defense) say 'there's a murderer out there' but they won't let me have a witness to find out."

I had a let down feeling. I needed a soft, feminine shoulder to lean on, someone to talk to, someone to help me let out all of my pent up feelings. The soft voice on the other end of the telephone assured me that I had the right person.

"Kris it's all over. The jury dismissed the case. The charges are dropped," I said.

"I'm sorry, we were both hoping the verdict would go the other way."

"Well it still can be appealed you know."

"Or it could end up in Civil Court with damages assessed," she said.

"That might be tough to prove, now that the charges are dismissed," I said.

There was a pause as both of us were caught up in our thoughts.

"Look, Mike, I know this case has been blowing your mind.

Why don't you come over for a cocktail? Then we'll have something light for dinner and unwind. I think you want to talk about it, am I right?"

"I was hoping you would ask. Might I also suggest that we try some dancing afterwards? I know a little place near Pontiac. They've got a terrific band. It's sort of out of the way and you can actually dance without getting a shoe in your shin. It'll do us both good."

"The way I look at it you need it more than I do, but I'm game."

"Good. See you in about 20 minutes."

I entered the apartment and the smell of Pizza in the oven greeted me as the door opened. There were two drinks on the cocktail table and the stereo was playing the "Big Band" sound.

As we crunched pistachios and sipped our drinks a warm, comfortable glow came over us like the anticipation pleasure before a pleasant happening. Suddenly the conversation was loose, uncluttered, relaxed, stimulating. It went to a subject familiar to both of us, the Furman trial. Somehow it always seemed to skirt our talk, hovering like an eagle above its mountain top nest.

At first we talked only of the basics, the blood/alcohol readings, the autopsy controversy and such and then we got into conclusions and feelings.

"You know," I said. "I think the jury's decision might have been technically correct but I can't help feeling that somewhere along the line society, life responsibility or whatever you want to call it, has been jilted. It's like you know something is morally bad but the law looks on it as technically correct and legal. If there had been some eyewitness accounts if there was some means of positive identification of the voice on the CB radio—all the evidence was heavily weighed towards circumstantial, not hard evidence. And the witnesses all seemed to have conflicting stories."

"I gathered that from reading your articles." she said. "The attorney, Hatcher, was quick on the pickup and brilliant in delivery. I keep going back to his statement 'somewhere out there is a murderer floating around.'"

"Was there? Or was it just his way of emotionalizing things, pushing the drama button, feeding 'soap box' oratory to an audience that seemed turned on by this approach. I don't know. Maybe he was playing on their ego or maybe it was the ham in him."

"I think it was 'ham.' Our lab reports showed no evidence of foul play."

"And yet he injected just enough uncertainty to make his theory believable, the fat lip, the bruises, the jeans pulled down over the buttocks. He painted a realistic picture."

"Along with some crackpot bull. That business of 'concussive effect.' It would be a miracle to pull a concussion out of a fist in the mouth. Tommy would have had to backpedal, strike something hard, and there's only sketchy evidence on that. It could have happened if he were thrown on the cement when they took him outside but they said they laid him down, not threw him down, so that's out. I don't know he could have gotten a concussion from a fist. The skull is one of the toughest parts of the human body. It's basic med school doctrine."

"You speak of controversy," I said. "What about the Hypothermia theory? It sounds way out, throwing off your clothes in 30–degree weather. And doesn't it contradict with Dr. Jenkins' testimony that in cold weather the mind keeps sending messages to the body to do something about the cold, in other words not throwing off clothes, but putting them on."

"I know," she said, "it's very confusing. I don't know how anyone can come up with a sensible decision. Even the factor of so many people coming and going and not being able to pinpoint anyone in the group of 20 to 25 young adults who saw Tommy wander off."

"It all goes back to the law again. I think we need laws that have teeth in them on adult responsibility. It's just too easy for young people to get their way with illegal booze. There's always a guy around who'll be the 'Good Joe.' No one wants the 'Bad Guy' label but maybe it's time to change labels, emphasize the point that the 'bad guy' can become the 'good guy.'

We both took sips. The thoughts were hitting home. It was too late to do anything now, I thought but in my mind I saw interviews coming up with judges, youth counselors and juvenile officers. Maybe I could make people aware of what was going on. It was worth a try.

"Enough of this serious discussion, it's time for dancing."

"I'm ready. We'll eat our pizzas and go."

It was a beautiful cold winter night. The moon was in the full stage. The air was crisp and clean. The snow crunched softly under the boot, scattering little fluffs of it right and left as you walked. Our breaths made patterns of icy vapor that blew back and bit at us. Our laughing voices were sharp and clean in the cold, frost–filled air.

I pulled the Mustang into the driveway of a bungalow type building with a flashing neon sign "Martin's Nest." The proprietor, Joe Martin, knew how to make a play on words.

It was a typical Friday evening at the "Nest." A four–piece band was laying on a rendition of "Misty." The moaning sax gave the song a blues touch while the drummer with a couple of 'fly swatters' was giving the tune a soft rhythmic background. An electronic organ made alternately like a flute, a trumpet and a piano. About six or seven couples were reacting to the music in different styles of dancing. One was doing a slow jitterbug, another a type of disco with all kinds of pretzel arm movements while another was just slow dancing, the man's hands noticeably placed on the lower extremity of the woman's back.

At the bar there was plenty of action. All of the barstools were filled with the single crowd. The conversation was animated as the men laid enticements of free drinks hoping to make it into some lady's boudoir that night. Like many taverns there was just enough light present to vaguely see who was sitting at the next table but not enough to make out their features. A young man approached a woman at a nearby table. He looked at her and quickly moved away. She was in the over sixty bracket. He walked back to his place at the bar, a sullen look on his face.

The "Nest" was one of my favorite drinking and dancing places. It was getting difficult to find any more places where live bands "with a beat" were playing. Always, it seemed, the modern bands emitted high pitched electronic music, "faceless" sounds of maddening tempos, screeching, twangy guitars that literally tore your eardrums apart. The other side were the DJ's who intermittently rolled the sound down to 40 decibels while they rent the air with blubbering, unintelligible pieces of uninteresting tidbits such as "All right out there you guys and gals, we're going to give you a little Jive now, J–I–V–E, so you guys get your favorite gal and do your thing. One, two, three, four."

And so on.

At the "Nest," thank God, this type of music had been given proper burial rites and entombed. Once in a while a venture–some manager resurrected this style but the emptiness of the floor and the solitary one or two couples that were courageous enough to brave the cold stares of those at the tables made such music unprofitable and it was banished to the high set at the Holiday Inns and the Sheraton Hotels.

We sat down and ordered our favorite drinks as the band swung into a mellow arrangement of "Feelings." The music was soft and slow, just right for slow dancing.

Even before our drinks arrived we were out on the dance floor. We danced and neither of us talked. Our bodies fused in a melody of sensuousness, love and caring.

Her cheek found mine. My arm tightened around her waist. Her hand found its way to the back of my head as our bodies drew close.

It could have been a beautiful and loving dream but it was reality, wonderful, warm reality, pushing out the hurt and inhumanity of a 15–year–old young man lying cold and dead in a frozen field.